The Magic Dozen at Emerald Pond

by Steve Brown
and Amber Sellers

Illustrated by Bob Commander

For volume or special orders please call 801-466-4272

ISBN: 978-0-9762800-3-3
Cover Art: Dave Thompson
Illustrations: Bob Commander
Book layout: Aucutt Design and Studio J Art Design

The Magic Dozen at Emerald Pond is published by Monkeyfeather Books, LLC

Be The Ball, Inc.
5711 Holladay Blvd.
Salt Lake City, UT 84121
www.betheballinc.com

Monkeyfeather Books, LLC
PO Box 520126
Salt Lake City, Utah 84152
www.mikeandthebike.com

BE THE BALL.

MONKEYFEATHER
BOOKS

BLUE
STAR

Dedication

Because Steve never takes no for an answer:

>I would like to dedicate this book to my husband, Joshua, who has the tiresome job of keeping me focused. You're my favorite.

>Thank you, Mason and Jasmine, for never ceasing to amaze me.

>A special thanks to my girls (Mom, Rachel, Amy, Ronnette, and Heidi). Without you loving my kids, I never could have finished this book...

A big hug and kiss to everyone who believed in magic golf balls, before their story was ever told.

— Amber

This book is dedicated to all the children *and* adults who continue to overcome life's challenges by believing in themselves and their abilities.

—Brown

Acknowledgments

Steve and Amber would like to acknowledge and thank the following people and/or families for their contributions and support. Without them, our book would never have become a reality.

Maggie Pratt
Kevin and Vicki Plumb
The Dean Austin Family
Jim Taggart
Liza Cozad
Rachel West
Gillian Rose Barnes
Bryan and Marlene Daybell
Mike and Beth Brown
Phil and Wendi Davies
Dee and Tami Young
Shirley K. Good
David D. Bettger
Brad and Rita LaVoie
Jim and Cindy Sellers

An additional "Thanks" is in order for the following longtime supporters of Be the Ball:

Nicole Jeray
Art and Gerry Barnes
Jeanne Brown
Matt and Melinda Frandsen
Ted Vickey
George Francisco
Jane and Steve Spicer
Frank LaRosa
Kevin and Jamie Zenger
Art and Deb Miyazaki
Larry Harmon
Dr. John Stohl
Patrick Ritter
Larry McLeod
The Cary Nichols Family
Ken Kurtz
Jeff Jagmin and Sherri Levin
Jeri Guss

Contents

The "Dozen" 2

Glossary 3

Chapter 1: A "Pinging" Shoelace 5

Chapter 2: Find the Key 10

Chapter 3: "Abra Kadabra" 16

Chapter 4: "Look Around, I've Brought my Friends" 23

Chapter 5: No Quick Fix 31

Chapter 6: "What Do You See?" 41

Chapter 7: "Call 911" 48

Chapter 8: A Gracious Offer 58

Chapter 9: Remember THIS! 68

Chapter 10: "What's Your Game Plan?" 76

Chapter 11: The Locker Room 83

Chapter 12: "Truth" 91

About the Authors 99

The "Magic Dozen"

Magic Dozen: The magical cast of golf balls who dedicate themselves to helping.

 Linx: Otherwise known as "Dude of the Dozen." The leader of the Magic Dozen.

 Beach: Surfer personality; spends most of his time in his lawn chair basking in the sun.

 Wet: Very environmentally conscious. Wherever water can be found, Wet will be found in it.

 Lost: Military in nature; prides himself in his ability to "know the way." Unfortunately, his sense of direction is misguided.

 Triple Bogey: A group of three that are always causing trouble.

 Mulligan: Originally from Scotland, he is supportive and believes in second chances.

 Long Ball: Risky; loves to go "flying."

 Birdie: Sings and dances in a most theatrical fashion.

 You-Da-Man: Arrogant; only he can do it all.

 Greenie: Single-minded; focused on the task at hand.

 Teena: Outgoing, sassy little lady who has caught Linx's attention… (Teena will be featured in the next Magic Dozen book.)

Glossary

Linx's Golf Terms: Frequently Used Terms in "The Magic Dozen at Emerald Pond"

Back nine: Holes 10 through 18 on a golf course.

Birdie: A hole played one stroke under par.

Bogey: A hole played one stroke over par.

Bunker fairway: A hazard of sand or bare earth, usually located in a recessed depression.

Double bogey: A hole played two strokes over par.

Eagle: A hole played two strokes under par.

Fairway: The short grass on the hole between the tee and the green.

Front nine: Holes 1 through 9 on a golf course.

Green or putting green: The area of specially prepared grass around the hole, where putts are played.

Hazard: Physical part of the course such as water traps or sand, bunkers, and hills where it is very hard to play the ball.

Lie: The ground that the ball is resting on. "Good lies" include the fairway and the green, while bunkers, pine straw, and the rough are examples of "bad lies."

Mulligan: A free shot after a bad shot, usually off the tee. Not allowed by the rules and not practiced in tournaments, but commonly used with friends playing socially.

Out-of-bounds: The area designated as being outside the boundaries of the course.

Par: Abbreviation for "professional average result." Par is the number of shots (strokes) the experts think it should take a golfer to get the ball in the hole.

Putt: A shot played on the green, usually with a putter.

Putter: A golf club with a very low loft used to make the ball roll.

Rough: Grass that borders the fairway, where the grass is un-mown. Usually, the rough grass is taller than the fairway.

Stroke: Hitting the ball toward the hole.

Tee box: Specially prepared area, usually a grassy area, from which the first stroke for each hole is made.

Triple bogey: A hole played three strokes over par.

Other Common Golf Terms

Aiming: The act of aligning the clubface to the target that the golfer intends the ball to go to.

Address: When a golfer adjusts his stance, positions himself relative to the ball, and begins the pre-swing routine.

Alignment: The position of a golfer's body in relation to the target of the ball.

Balance: The correct distribution of the golfer's weight at address and throughout the swing.

Ball marker: Any small object used to mark where a player's ball is on the green. Some golfers use coins as ball markers.

Caddie: A person paid to carry a player's clubs and offer advice.

Cart: 1) Electrical vehicle used to transport players from hole to hole. 2) Hand-pulled cart to carry a bag of clubs (usually has wheels).

Chip: A short shot that travels through the air over a very short distance and rolls the rest of the way to the hole. Usually played from extremely close to and around the green.

Clubface: The angled surface of the golf club head that is used to hit the ball. The center of the clubface is known as the "sweet spot." To maximize distance and accuracy, players should hit the ball with the center of the clubface.

Clubhouse: The clubhouse is the golfer's source for information about local rules, the conditions of the course, and other essential information for the avid golfer. Generally, golfers can also purchase balls, clubs, and other golfing equipment at the clubhouse.

Divot: A notch (chunk of grass) caused by the clubhead hitting the ground several inches before the ball.

Fore: A warning that is shouted when it appears possible that a ball may hit other players or spectators.

Line: The expected path of the ball to get into the hole. Other golfers must never "step in a player's line" on the green.

Links: A course along the ocean, usually devoid of trees and therefore windy. So named because courses beside the sea were often the link between the beach and farmland. Many courses in the United Kingdom are links.

Pitch: A short shot (typically from within 50 yards), usually made using a less than full swing, to flight the ball towards the hole.

Short game: Shots, such as putting, chipping, pitching, and bunker play, that usually take place on or near the green.

Tee: A small piece of equipment, made of wood or plastic, placed in the teeing ground. The golf ball is placed upon the tee prior to the first stroke on a hole.

1

A "Pinging" Shoelace

Mr. Manning stared at Mason with the look that kids talked about in the cafeteria. The one that made you lose your appetite. The one that made you think your life was over. The one that said, "I will deal with your friends after I call your parents." Mason swallowed hard. He could feel his stomach doing flip-flops as his hands started to go numb...

"Maybe you'd like to explain in your own words why you and your friends thought it was okay to tease A.J." said Principal Manning.

As Mason stood, struggling with what his response should be, it occurred to him that he really couldn't think of a good reason. Finally, after accepting that no answer would be good enough, he decided to give the only answer he knew.

"It's just that...um, it's just that he really wants to play basketball with us." *It's not my fault that AJ's not any good. Tony's the one who told him he could play today. Mr. Manning would have laughed too if he had seen AJ grab the ball, run onto the court, and trip as soon as he got there.*

"After he fell, everyone just laughed, is that correct?" questioned the principal.

Afraid to get himself deeper into trouble, Mason figured fewer words were better. "Um, I...I guess so." The truth was that it had been the hardest Mason had laughed in a long time. It had been really funny.

This was not good. "My parents are out of town for the weekend. I'm s'posed to go home with Tony after school," Mason said quickly.

He was going to have the best sleepover ever! They were going to play video games, rent a movie, and maybe even make popcorn and sleep in the fort they made in Tony's backyard.

"Who is watching you for the rest of the weekend?" Principal Manning asked.

"My grandpa," whispered Mason. Grandpa was "Pops" to Mason, but "Colonel" to the rest of the world. Mason knew how Pops felt about teasing. This weekend could turn into a disaster with just one phone call.

As he walked through the echoing halls of his school toward the office, Mason could hear the shoelace of his untied shoe pinging against the cement floor with each step. The firm grasp Principal Manning had on his shoulder told him this was not the time to bother with his shoelace.

Minutes later, waiting outside the office while Mr. Manning talked with Pops was the worst thing that could have happened to Mason on this otherwise perfect Friday afternoon.

"Your grandpa is on his way to pick you up. Return to class and get your things," directed Mr. Manning.

Again, Mason's stomach flipped, threatening to give back the turkey sandwich he had eaten for lunch. What would the Colonel do? Hopefully Mason's mother had not given him any ideas before she left.

Mason finally sat down outside next to the flagpole. He knew only one thing could be taking Pops so long. He was perfecting his punishment. He would be taking the television out of the room that belonged to Mason when he stayed the night. No doubt the video games would be hidden away. Mason imagined an empty spot where the dish of his favorite taffy was always waiting for him on the coffee table.

The hardest thing would be the woods. Pops would see to it that Mason didn't set foot outside. He had planned on hiking, climbing, and scouting around like he did every time he visited Pops, but not this time.

He was sure of one thing. The Colonel would make him suffer for the teasing he had done. Everyone called Pops "Colonel" because he had been in the Air Force. He had probably been taught special detention tactics. Tactics that Mason didn't want to know about…

Finally, the rumbling from Pops' blue Chevy Silverado interrupted Mason's thoughts. He walked over to the passenger-side door and hoisted himself up into the seat. Sheepishly, he looked at his grandpa, "Hey Pops…"

"Hello Mason…it seems we have a problem."

The rest of the ride was silent. Pops was not one for lecturing when he got angry. He was more of the silent type, leaving one to wonder what he was thinking. As they rounded the last corner and pulled into the driveway, Mason could see the enormous trees looming from behind Pops' huge house. *Too bad I won't be spending any time there this weekend.*

Everything about Pops was big. Not just his house, and the woods that accompanied it, but his shoes were bigger than any Mason had ever seen before. One time when Mason was younger he had been wrestling with Pops when Pops grabbed the top of his head, palming it like a basketball. It was at that moment Mason decided he really didn't ever want to make him angry. Even though he was a soft-spoken and kind man, his sheer size would cause anybody to think twice before ignoring his directions.

The truck stopped. Mason could feel Pops staring at him. Without a word Pops got out and walked toward his house. Mason sat quietly. Should he get out? Should he just wait to see what Pops wanted him to do next? After about five minutes, Mason decided Pops might just leave him in the truck for the weekend if he didn't get out on his own. Quickly he went inside and headed straight to his room hoping to delay his punishment.

When he opened the door he saw his TV. Must be that Pops wanted it to hurt a little worse by removing it in front of him. *Just how angry is Pops?*

An hour later, Pops walked into Mason's room and set a plate of cookies between them and handed Mason a glass of milk. Should he say something? Maybe he should try to make Pops laugh? Mason knew from previous experience that adults liked to hear the words, "I'm sorry." But Mason wasn't sorry. As far as he was concerned he had done nothing wrong. Why should he have to suffer because AJ was uncoordinated? After considering the possibilities, Mason decided he would let Pops break the silence.

Pops had eaten the last cookie before he asked, "How would you have felt if you were AJ?"

I am NOT AJ! How would I know what it feels like to be him? He had never been the last one to get chosen in a pickup game. Only one time had Mason been picked fourth by a team captain for basketball or baseball. He was usually second or third. He wasn't the very best, but he was definitely not the worst (and in his wildest dreams he would *never* have dropped his lunch tray in front of everyone).

"Um…I dunno. I'm sorry Pops. I didn't mean to make him feel bad." There, that had to be a safe answer.

Pops slowly nodded his head up and down. Mom would have been all over an apology like that, but the Colonel wasn't impressed.

"What if no one wanted you to play ball?" asked Pops.

"I guess I would just find my own friends."

Pops was silent. Again, the only response was a slight nod of his head. Mason saw the window of opportunity open slightly. No punishment yet.

"What is AJ like?" Pops asked.

Mason hated when grownups asked questions like this. AJ was clumsy! He was annoying! He was the smallest one in class. Mason didn't know much more than that about him, and he didn't want to.

"Pops, I don't really like him. It's his fault that I'm not at Tony's…he ruins everything! Nobody likes him!" The words landed hard on the bed between Mason and Pops. As soon as they left his mouth, Mason knew it was a mistake. He wished he could inhale deeply and take them back.

Pops stared out the window. "How do you know?"

"Um…I just do," Mason mumbled. He knew there would be no fixing what he had said. He had blurted it out in frustration, and now he would have to suffer the consequences.

"All right, it's settled then," said Pops. He got up and left the room.

What was "settled"? That word didn't sit well with Mason. He didn't know what Pops meant. *Am I going to be grounded all weekend? Is it going to get worse? Or, maybe it's over?* Mason wished he could disappear. If he could quietly keep to himself, he might somehow make it through this weekend. He stayed in his room where he helped himself to the remote once he was sure Pops wasn't coming back. After a few hours Mason stepped out of his room and saw Pops sitting on the back porch reading the paper. He grabbed a cherry taffy as he walked through the living room. Then, he headed out to see Hammer.

Hammer was Pops' big, black and white mutt. He attacked Mason, licking his arms and panting his bad, doggy breath in his face. Mason threw the ball a few times for him before he was called to dinner.

Dinner was silent. Mason began to worry all over again. Immediately after eating Pops told Mason it was time for bed. A quick peek outside showed it was still bright and beautiful. It could've been a lot worse. He got ready for bed, pulled back the covers, and let his head fall back onto his pillow. Oh well, at least it didn't appear that he was grounded. Going to bed early was better than losing all of his privileges.

In the middle of the night, and in the middle of a weird dream, Mason felt Pops' hand on his shoulder. "Get up son, grab your shoes. I have something I'd like to show you."

"My shoes? Where are we going?" Mason questioned groggily.

"You'll see."

"What time is it?"

"Early."

After slipping his shoes on he looked down at his green and yellow plaid pajama shirt. Next, his eyes shifted to his green and yellow plaid matching shorts. These had been his mother's choice. He could hear Pop's Silverado rumbling in the driveway. Dark or not, Mason wasn't going to leave the house dressed like this. If he had been wearing his Star Wars sleep shirt and black matching shorts, the thought of changing wouldn't have crossed his mind. But, as it was, he quickly took off his shoes, and slipped on his jean shorts. He pulled his favorite tee shirt over his spiky brown hair and high tailed it to the truck. Once again, Pops was silent.

Mason decided it was best not to pressure Pops about where they were going. The last thing he wanted was to get into another discussion about AJ. Then, after almost 40 minutes—according to Mason's brand new silver and black, shatterproof, water-resistant, digital watch—Pops pulled into a parking lot on the edge of town. It no longer felt like the middle of the night. With each second the sky seemed to brighten. As soon as the truck stopped, a man in a golf cart came buzzing over and opened Pops' door.

"Good morning, Colonel," said the man.

"Good morning, Arnie."

It seemed Pops was a regular. Mason knew he liked golf. Pops started walking over to a large grove of trees. Underneath the trees was a big wooden bench. On the way, two men with silver hair waved. The Colonel gave a casual salute. Nobody here seemed to be under a hundred years old, except for Pops…and Mason of course.

"Let's settle here for a while," Pops said as he patted the bench. "I brought you here to tell you the story of a boy named Zack."

There it was. The punishment! Pops was going to bore him to death. That's what had been "settled." Mason groaned inwardly. *If this is going to be the punishment, then let's get this show on the road.*

"Did you know him, Pops?"

"Once upon a time I did."

2

Find the Key

"Zack was a nice kid," Pops began. "But he had no friends. He was rounder, shorter, and quieter than most. The kids at school picked on him, teachers really didn't notice him, and schoolwork rarely made much sense to him. He was sure he wasn't smart or funny. He believed he wasn't good at much, and Zack was not alone in his thinking. Zeppelin Zack, Triple Chin, and Jelly Belly were just a few of his nicknames."

Mason smothered a laugh. Those were pretty good. Pops slid a sideways glance at him. Mason immediately erased the smile from his face.

Very few things made Zack happy, but golf was one of them. Zack worked at the local golf driving range, where he washed practice balls. Once a landmark of the town, touring professionals would stop by to perfect their skills and offer clinics for the locals. Golfers, young and old, would come by hoping to meet the famous players and gather autographs.

But, time had taken its toll on the range. The newer, modern practice facility across town had lured the business away. Zack didn't mind; he liked the quiet. It was the sound of the occasional crisp click of a club hitting the ball that kept him coming back for more.

One day, in the golf ball washroom, Zack was listening to the golf balls in the washer and staring at the walls. They were covered with photographs and posters of all the great players from the last 50 years. One poster in particular was Zack's favorite. It was a framed poster of Ben Hogan. As far as Zack was concerned, Ben Hogan was the greatest golf player that ever lived. The lullaby rhythm of the washer lulled Zack into a familiar daydream, that someday he would be one of the players in the posters. Then reality intruded.

"Well, well, well, Ol' Jelly Roll is doing his laundry. Hey, Fat Boy! Get me a bucket of balls!" Standing at the counter was Johnny Beam. Johnny and his henchmen had made Zack the target of their teasing since first grade.

Zack avoided looking at Johnny. His safe haven had been discovered. *Why does he have to play here? Isn't seeing him at school enough?* Zack simply filled a bucket and handed it over.

Turning, Johnny yelled, "Hey, Jelly Belly Roll, come watch how the real players hit!"

Johnny tried to show off his years of private lessons. Zack thought he must be the best junior player in the city by now. Zack watched as Johnny took his stance and pulled the club back to his shoulder. At first it seemed to be all textbook perfection, but something was missing.

After cleaning four more batches of golf balls, Zack peered out the washroom window hoping to see that Johnny and company had left. The boys were huddled together talking. Zack had been in this situation before. Something bad was about to happen to somebody. And it was usually him.

Zack ducked back into the washroom, thankful for the solitude. He began to dry off the washed balls when a sizzling sound buzzed past his ear. Zack looked around to see a bouncing range ball slowing to a roll. Suddenly from the corner of his eye, something caught his attention. That "something" was speeding toward him. Quickly he hit the floor, catching a glimpse of another ball bouncing off the wall and then the ceiling of the washroom. Shouted insults flew at him at the same rate of speed as the golf balls.

"Hey, Belly Boy, we've seen your swing in gym class. Don't you think you'd be able to swing the club better if your gut wasn't in the way? You're better for target practice than you could ever be at playing golf!" Johnny drew back his club and sent another ball soaring through the air towards Zack, while the other boys held the washer room door open.

Soon Zack found himself in a hailstorm of golf balls. He crawled into a corner, covered his head, and hoped not to get hit. Glass was shattering, walls were denting, and the sound was deafening. Zack felt a sting on his right shoulder. One of the balls had found its mark. Zack fought the desire to panic. *Whack!* One of the balls had ricocheted off the floor and pelted him in the shin.

"HEY, STOP IT! GET OUT AND DON'T COME BACK!!!"

One more ball was sent sailing through the air before he heard the sound of tennis shoes retreating in the opposite direction. Zack slowly stood up. He knew the voice.

"Zack, are you okay?" questioned Mr. Vogel as he stormed through the door. "Are you hurt?"

"I don't know," Zack replied sheepishly. He could feel a welt beginning to form on his shoulder.

"It's okay now Zack, they're gone," said Mr. Vogel as he turned from the door.

Mason interrupted Pops' story. "I wouldn't have ever done that. Zack's not cool, but they don't have to hurt him."

"Golf balls aren't the only things that hurt, Mason..." That was all Pops said before he continued on with his story.

Mr. Vogel checked Zack over. The welts were the only physical damage. They were turning bright red. He had the one on his shoulder, one on his back, and a large knot on his shin. "You will have some big bruises tomorrow; this one will be a beauty." said Mr. Vogel pointing to Zack's shin, trying to make him laugh. "Did you know those kids?"

Zack took a deep breath and thought for a moment. "No." It was a better answer than saying yes and having to suffering later at the hands of Johnny Beam.

"Are you sure?"

"Yes, I'm sure," said Zack as he looked away.

Mr. Vogel didn't look convinced, but didn't ask any more questions. "Well then, let's start cleaning up."

Mr. Vogel had owned the driving range since the beginning. He had been a touring pro and traveled the country playing with all the great players. Because of an injury, he had given up the tour. He never looked back and seemed to have no regrets. He enjoyed the range and especially loved teaching. He was full of stories from the "good ol' days." His laugh was infectious, his smile friendly.

Time and travel had begun to take their toll on Mr. Vogel's body. He had recently started keeping his 4 iron with him. It was clear by the way he used it when he walked that he needed it to get around. His favorite club had gone from helping him make great shots, to helping him walk. Once Zack had referred to it as a cane and had received a quick reminder that it most definitely was not a cane. It was his "trusty 4 iron," and nothing more.

Mr. Vogel wasn't a large man. Though Zack hadn't noticed, Mr. Vogel had grown thinner over the last few years, and the pain in his back had forced him to hunch over ever so slightly. Mr. Vogel had a full head of silvery hair. He may have lost a few things in his lifetime, but his hair was not one of them. Mr. Vogel always smelled of sunscreen because of the thick layer he put on each morning. He believed that keeping the sun off his face was the key to never, "growing up or growing old."

Mr. Vogel loved Zack and treated him like a son. Often times after Zack was finished for the day, Mr. Vogel would practice with him on the driving range. He saw raw, hidden talent in Zack where others saw nothing.

"Be careful of the glass, Zack." Mr. Vogel warned. As he stepped over the broken pieces, Zack surveyed the number of golf balls that had been flung at him. He considered himself lucky that only three had hit him. *Maybe it isn't target practice that Johnny needs. Maybe it's a better swing…*

Zack was carefully picking up shards of glass when he looked at his favorite picture of Ben Hogan, now tilted and barely hanging on the wall. He carefully touched the inscription in the bottom right hand corner. It read, "Keep up the good work V." Underneath the inscription was a signature, *Henny Bogen.* Zack had heard from Mr. Vogel's customers that it really was written by Ben Hogan. Rumor had it that he would sometimes sign this way, making close friends and family laugh. Zack wasn't sure if he believed that or not. Others said that Mr. Vogel just wrote it himself.

A round hole could be seen where a ball had torn the paper. Zack slowly slid his hand up the picture and placed his finger in the hole. His finger went into the hole without feeling a solid wall behind it. Next he put his whole fist through, but could not feel anything…just emptiness.

Zack lifted the picture off the wall, finding a much larger hole. He reached in to recover the damaging golf ball. What his hand found was anything but a golf ball! He felt the smooth, dusty edge of a rectangular object under his fingers. He began to run his hand along the edge, trying to figure out what it was.

"Mr. Vogel," shouted Zack. "I found something hidden in the wall!"

"What is it Zack?"

"I don't know. I'm trying to reach it."

Zack pulled a chair over to the wall, climbed on top, and put his whole arm into the hole. Grabbing the corner of the box, he carefully lifted it through the wall.

"Take it slow and easy," said Mr. Vogel who appeared to be almost as excited as Zack.

The box was dusty and held together with a rubber band. The rubber band had been twisted and wrapped back around so that it held all four sides. Neatly tucked underneath the rubber band was an envelope. Zack and Mr. Vogel stared at the box in amazement. Questions silently filled their minds. It didn't look like anything special. Zack knew that if it had been on one of the storeroom shelves, he never would have thought twice about what was inside. But it wasn't on the shelf…it was *in* the wall.

"Shall we take a look?" asked Mr. Vogel.

Zack tried to carefully pull the stiff rubber band off the box. It was clear the rubber band had lost its "rubber." As Zack was sliding it off, it broke. There was no snap. The envelope fell to the floor. Zack picked it up and handed it to Mr. Vogel. Mr. Vogel held both of his hands up and shook his head.

"Oh no Zack, you found it, you open it." With unstable fingers Zack tore open the envelope.

"What does it say?" A single card was inside with only a few handwritten lines.

Zack was embarrassed. Reading was just one of the many things Zack was *not* good at. He had gotten good at hiding his secret from most people, and he didn't feel like now was a good time for Mr. Vogel to find out. Zack slowly and deliberately tried to sound out its message. Stuttering along he read:

These balls are magical,
if you can find the key.
I only hope they teach you
as much as they taught me.
H.B.

"What does it mean? Who's HB?" Zack asked. *Could it possibly be that one of the greatest players of all time left this box for me to find? No way!*

"When I first opened the range, professional golfers from the tour used to come over and help me drum up business. Ben Hogan did stop by on occasion," Mr. Vogel said as he stared at the box. "Could Ben have pulled a fast one on me?"

"Could it really be his initials?" asked Zack.

"Um...I, um, maybe," was all that Mr. Vogel could say.

As he sat there with the box in his hands, Zack's imagination took over. If he was in fact holding balls, which were magical, from Ben Hogan; then life could get interesting! Magical myths and legends swirled through his mind. *Could this be like a genie-in-the-bottle? I know exactly what I'll wish for...*

Of course, he would begin with the obvious things. He would wish Johnny Beam out of his life forever. He would wish he had friends at school and that he would never get picked on again by anyone. It might also help if he wasn't living in the old, small, dingy apartment at 381 Dead End Drive. And, to top off his new, perfect life, he'd wish for tons of money, so his mom would never have to work again.

He could even see himself walking down the fairway of the eighteenth hole of Augusta, soon to become the youngest player ever to win the Masters golf tournament. With each stride he could hear his name being chanted by the thousands of fans who created a corridor leading directly to the green. He waved and tipped his cap. After his final putt, the tournament would be his. He was soon escorted to the cabin where the green jacket was being slipped over his shoulders. Mr. Vogel's voice interrupted Zack's imaginary fame.

"Zack, are you going to open the box?"

"Um...yeah."

"Hurry up, I want to see what 'magic' golf balls look like, and I'm not getting any younger!"

Zack slid to the ground, sitting cross-legged on the cold floor. Mr. Vogel sat on the chair that Zack had used to reach the box. Before taking off the lid he paused, wondering too what they would look like. Would they be shining…no, glowing? He thought for just a second about the best looking golf balls he had ever seen, and wondered if they would even compare to the ones he was holding right now.

Finally, with one deep breath, Zack lifted the lid off of the box. He and Mr. Vogel's mouths dropped open. Zack threw the lid aside and stared into the box. Never before had he seen anything like this. The balls were incredible, that was for sure!

"Look at these!" said Mr. Vogel, as he reached in and picked up one of the golf balls. "Well, kid, this is the last thing I expected to see, how about you?"

Zack said nothing.

3

"Abra Kadabra"

It was unbelievable. Inside the box were 12 of the filthiest, most scuffed up, sliced golf balls Zack had ever seen. He was used to range balls, which were forever getting marked up and dingy. These were worse. Some even had pieces of dirt and grass still clinging to them. It was obvious that they had never seen the inside of a washer. Yet, each ball had been carefully placed inside the box. A cardboard divider separated each ball from the others. Zack thought it strange that they would be packaged so neatly, considering their condition.

Zack lifted one ball out of the box and began to turn it over and over in his hand, examining the entire surface. He brushed the dirt away, looking for a label. After inspecting the first ball thoroughly he put it down and grabbed another. Neither of the first two balls had any identifying mark. Zack had never seen a ball free of advertisement. Every golf ball he had ever seen had some kind of logo, usually sporting a company name or the golf ball manufacturer. It seemed odd… but for that matter, so had this whole experience.

Finally, after finding his voice, just slightly above a whisper, Zack asked, "Why does this note say they are magical?"

"I don't know. Maybe they *were,* or maybe someone thought it would be a great prank. It's hard to say."

"What are we going to do with them?" Zack asked as he and Mr. Vogel continued to inspect each ball.

Mr. Vogel set the last ball back in its place, "Well, I believe they belong to you. Whatever you'd like to do with them is fine with me. You found them, so I think you should keep them. Besides, you've got the welts to prove that you've earned them." Mr. Vogel said with a wink and a quick pat on Zack's *good* shoulder.

"Why don't you try cleaning them up a little? Couldn't hurt." Mr. Vogel offered. *Right, like that's going to make a difference…no one ever said the washer was magical!*

Zack began by taking all the other balls out of the washer. He wasn't going to take the chance of mixing these balls up with the others. Inside the washer he could hear them clicking against each other.

When the washer was finished he grabbed a drying bin. As he picked up the first ball, he noticed an improvement. This ball didn't look bad. He'd been sure that even after a good washing, they would still be awful. He set the first one in the drying bin and picked up another. The second ball looked as good as the first. *Is this actually working?*

After they were all in the drying bin, Zack decided to give them another whirl. Back in the washer they went. This time, when he picked up the first ball, he gasped. It was almost beautiful…but where had all the scuff marks gone? He decided to wash them a third time.

Zack went to find Mr. Vogel.

"You might want to come see this."

"What is it?"

"It…it's the balls," Zack stuttered. "They're just finishing their third cleaning."

When Zack and Mr. Vogel lifted the first ball out of the washer, neither knew what to say. Zack looked it over, the same as he had done when he had found them filthy inside the box. Mr. Vogel grabbed a couple of them out of the washer.

"I don't believe it Zack, what did you do?"

"Nothing. Just put them through the washer. I never thought they could get this clean. Where are the slices? What about all the scuff marks?" Zack didn't expect an answer.

"Well Zack, good job. It looks like they just needed a little tender loving care. You'd better start home before it gets any later. Those welts could probably use some care too." Zack had completely forgotten about his shoulder and his shin, and the welt on his back that Mr. Vogel hadn't seen. He packed the balls up and put them in his backpack for safekeeping.

Zack could see where the road curved to the left up ahead. He would follow the bend for a few blocks before he would arrive in front of his apartment building. He and his mother lived on the second floor. They were just two of the many people packed into the small structure. The street in front of their apartment came to a dead end less than a block away. A few other old houses, a ton of weeds, and some empty lots covered the stretch of road that belonged to Zack.

As he walked, Zack thought about how his mom worked two shifts almost every day. She was gone to work before he left for school. At some time during the day, she came home for a break between shifts while Zack was still at school. She left for her second shift before Zack got home. This meant that most nights Zack came home to an empty home. It had become routine for Zack to fall asleep on the couch, watching television. He liked the sound of voices in the room.

His mother would wake him when she came home. She was always there to tuck him in, and even though Zack would never let anyone know, this was his favorite part of the whole day. His mom would ask him about his day and what had happened at school, or at the driving range. Then, he would ask about her day. Together they played a game called the best of the worst. Each of them would take turns telling what the best part of their day was, and then sharing the worst. Tonight would be easy. The worst part of the day had become the best.

As he started up the stairs to his apartment, he was careful to avoid the left side. There was a large crack in the cement that had made him trip more times than he cared to admit. Inside, the hallway was narrow and the air was stuffy. After walking up two flights of stairs, Zack was winded.

He took out his keys and opened the door. He was surrounded by the smell of cookies. Today, as most days, his mother had made him an after school snack. It was usually cookies or brownies. Sometimes it was a bag of his favorite chips, and of course, a soda.

Next to the plate of cookies was a note from his mother, "Hope you had a good day, I'll see you tonight. Dinner's in the freezer. Love you, Mom." Zack walked over to the freezer, pulled it open, and stared at the pile of frozen dinners. Picking out his own each night used to be fun, but now that Zack had tried each one numerous times, the excitement was gone. His normal routine was to grab his snack, settle on the couch, and flip on the television.

Tonight was different. Zack went to his room and carefully put the box of balls on his bed. He slipped the letter out of the envelope and read the poem again.

These balls are magical,
if you can find the key.
I only hope they teach you
as much as they taught me.
H.B.

Zack stared at the initials. The writing was just like the signature on the poster. If they were magical, Zack was determined to find out about that key.

He read the poem out loud to the balls, as though he was a magician. Nothing happened. "Abra Kadabra!" he shouted as he pointed at the box. As soon as he said it, he felt stupid. *Forget it... This could never work!*

Zack wished he had brought home a putter so he could practice in the living room. If he moved the couch and pulled the coffee table out of the way, there was just enough room for him to putt.

He had never had any golf balls of his own. Maybe if these got used, they would release their magic. He was upset with himself for not thinking of it earlier. Now he would have to wait until tomorrow.

After dinner, instead of heading for the couch, he went to his room, laid on his bed, and began replaying the day's events. It wasn't until that moment that Zack realized he would have to face Johnny and his friends at school the next day. He hated the thought of what Johnny was going to do since Mr. Vogel had come to his rescue. Johnny had done other terrible things, but so far, this had been the worst.

Zack was still very intrigued by the balls, and wanted to spend his time thinking about the possibilities, but instead he was torn between excitement and fear for what tomorrow would hold. *Time to eat.*

He went into the kitchen and grabbed a bag of potato chips. As he sat on his bed, eating chips and thinking about the next day, a smile crossed his face. Tomorrow was Friday. *The day probably won't be good, but at least I'll have the weekend to myself…no Johnny.* For the first time in a long time, Zack fell asleep in his bed instead of on the couch.

He awoke suddenly when he felt his mother's weight against the mattress as she sat next to him. She leaned over and tousled his hair, then kissed his cheek. Zack opened his eyes slightly, confused by his surroundings. "What's goin' on honey?" his mother asked softly. "What are you doin' in your bed?" Zack looked around, amazed that he had fallen asleep without knowing it.

"I…I don't know. I guess I was just really tired." She laughed a little and then asked about his day. Should he tell her? She would definitely be upset by Johnny's attack. How would he explain the box of golf balls? Though he was excited, his mind was too clouded to think clearly. He decided if he was going to tell her, he'd do it later.

"It was okay. How was yours?" She quickly told him the highlights and lowlights of her day at work. He was hardly listening.

She picked up on his distant stare and said, "I'm goin' to let you get some sleep. See you tomorrow…same time, same place?"

"Yep, love you."

"I love you too." She whispered as she slipped out of his room and leaned the door shut behind her. Within seconds, Zack's body had relaxed into his sheets, and he was headed for his own personal dreamland.

Zack's alarm buzzed at 6:30. He had set the box of balls on his nightstand the night before, with the lid closed tightly. Before his feet even hit the floor he took off the lid to look at his beautiful, almost new, and possibly magic, golf balls.

He lifted a few of them out of the box, one at time, inspecting them for any signs of change. Nothing had happened. Nothing. Down deep he had hoped that somehow the balls would have had a delayed reaction to his attempts at releasing their magic. He put the balls in his backpack and got ready for school.

Zack walked carefully down the steps of his apartment building. He was going to wear shorts, until he saw how large the bruise had gotten on his shin and decided to wear long pants instead. The last thing he wanted to do was to display Johnny's work. The sun was shining, but the air was still crisp and cooler than Zack expected.

He could feel the knot in his stomach getting tighter as he thought about seeing Johnny. There was little doubt that something awful would be waiting for him as he began the day. Johnny would have had plenty of time to plan something since he had been chased off by Mr. Vogel. The whole class would probably hear that Zack was a tattletale, even though he wasn't the one who alerted Mr. Vogel. No one would hear his side, just Johnny's.

The walk to school for Zack was a little farther than the walk to the driving range. Zack would rather have taken the bus, but two of the guys in Johnny's crew took the bus. In the past, they had used this time to test their bullying skills. Johnny would have been proud of them. Two years had gone by since Zack vowed that he had taken his last ride on the school bus. Either way, school wasn't too far, and this morning especially, Zack was thankful that walking took him a little more time than riding the bus.

The bell rang and all the kids ran towards the school building. Zack was not in so much of a hurry. He kept walking, keeping one eye open and searching over his shoulder, as the other one scanned the scene up ahead. The last thing he wanted was to have Johnny sneak up on him.

He didn't see Johnny until he reached the classroom. Zack quickly walked in, without making eye contact, and settled into his seat. Zack put his backpack on the floor, safely placed between his feet.

The morning started off with a really long English lesson. Zack hated this subject most of all. He sat rigid in his seat, hoping and praying that his teacher would not call on him. He never raised his hand. He constantly found himself looking around the room to see if other hands were in the air. If they were, he could relax for a moment, until another question was asked.

Finally, it was time for history. He didn't love history, but it was better than English. His class had been studying the Civil War. To begin the lesson, Mrs. Korey asked the class, "Who remembers the name of the battle in the Civil War, which is known as the war's turning point?"

Zack lifted his head to look at his teacher. *I know the answer? I never know the answer.* It was either because he didn't pay enough attention, or just because he wasn't that smart, but Zack had never before felt confident that he could answer one of Mrs. Korey's questions.

His eyes scanned the room as the reality set in that no one else was raising their hand. Should he do it? He was positive that he had the right answer. A wrong answer would be tragic, but he felt sure of himself. Timidly, he held his hand up no higher than his head. At first Mrs. Korey didn't notice. Then she looked straight at him.

"Zack…go ahead."

"Um, it's uh, the Battle of Gettysburg." Zack stammered.

"Yes, yes it is. Great job."

Zack didn't recognize this feeling. His body felt light, and he had to fight the urge to laugh. It was incredible.

Something caught his eye. Did his bag move? He picked up his backpack and unzipped one side. Then, he reached his hand in and felt for the box. The lid was still on. He lifted it and peered inside to see that each ball was still perfectly in its place. Nothing had happened. Maybe his mind had played a trick on him while he was caught up in his earlier excitement…or maybe not. Regardless, Zack would remember this moment for a long time.

Before he replaced the lid, his fingers felt the dimpled surface of one of the balls. He curled his hand around it, pulled it out, and slid it into his pocket.

After a quick math lesson, it was time for gym class. Again, this was not a strong point on Zack's list of strengths and weaknesses.

Johnny was in the accelerated gym class. Basically, it meant that while everyone else was working on skills like jumping rope and dribbling a basketball, Johnny got to practice golf. Because he was a junior tournament player, he was allowed to practice, instead of participate in whatever other skill the rest of the class was learning. Johnny had golf practice for an hour every other day. Zack wished he could be out in the field practicing.

From the outdoor basketball court, Zack could see Johnny taking swings with the other kids from the junior league. He watched as Johnny tried hard to hit his golf ball past the 175 yard red flag. Johnny was on his fifth attempt before Zack turned away and tried to focus on basketball.

Before he worked on his dribbling, he felt for the golf ball he had tucked safely into his jeans pocket. It was still there. As he dribbled the ball, he began to wonder if he could hit the ball past the red flag. What if he could hit the ball past the green flag, or maybe even out to the blue flag? Each color marked a further distance, and if the ball could reach the blue flag, Zack would have hit it 250 yards.

Lunch was right after gym class. *Maybe, if I didn't get caught, I could try to hit my ball out to the markers? Johnny always leaves his clubs, and he doesn't come back for them until after lunch…*

A half hour later, the gym teacher, Mr. Barnes, blew the whistle. It was time for lunch. Zack slowly walked over to the clubs, waiting for all the kids to go to the cafeteria. He knew he was probably forfeiting his safety for a chance to prove something to himself. *What was the worst that could happen?* Maybe he didn't want to think about that.

The sudden discovery of his courageous side thrilled him. This was another new experience. Twice in one day…he was on a roll. This would be his first chance to use one of the golf balls. He had almost made it to the bag, when he heard someone behind him yell.

"Hey Johnny, looks like Fat Boy is thinkin' about becomin' a golfer!" One of Johnny's stooges was letting him know that Zack was invading their territory. Zack cringed. At least he hadn't touched anything yet.

"Go ahead, Zack, just *try* and swing a club," shouted Johnny as he turned around and started back towards Zack.

"Just a minute you guys," said Mr. Barnes.

"We just don't think he can swing a club. But, if he wants to, he's welcome to use mine," said Johnny with a cruel grin.

"Hold on, there's no reason why Zack couldn't play golf. Are you any good son?" Mr. Barnes asked Zack.

"I don't know. I guess not. I just like to play." Zack replied hesitantly as he shrugged his shoulders.

"Well, go ahead, give it a try," encouraged Mr. Barnes.

4

"Look Around, I've Brought My Friends"

Zack looked over his shoulder to see where all the whispering was coming from. The other kids in his class must have seen Johnny running back over and decided to join him. Zack pulled out the driver, lined up his club, and perfected his stance. Before he took his swing, the one that everyone would be talking about no matter how it went, he thought about Mr. Vogel. *What would he say if he were here?* Zack could hear him saying things like, *"You're great! Let it fly! Forget about these kids, just do your best and focus."*

"Give me that. I'll show you! You have no idea," Johnny spouted as he grabbed the club out of Zack's hand and nudged him out of the way.

"Hold on there Johnny," said Mr. Barnes. "Each of you can take one swing, that's it."

Johnny lined himself up and took a few practice swings. When he finally hit the ball, Zack was relieved. It was, by all accounts, a terrible shot. The golf ball flew in a sort of lopsided arch. It caught the wind, sailed left, and stopped short in the grass way ahead of the red mark. "Okay Johnny, it's Zack's turn. Hand him the club," directed Mr. Barnes.

"No, I get one more shot. I wasn't ready!"

"One shot each, and then it's lunch time. What are you worried about anyway, I thought you said Zack couldn't play."

Johnny threw down the club and stepped back, daring Zack to try. Zack pulled the ball from his pocket and placed it on the tee. There had to be at least forty kids watching him, not to mention his gym teacher. Never before had so many eyes been on him. *Oh, this is just great. Everything tragic in my life happens in front of an audience.* Mentally he put himself next to Mr. Vogel, getting a driving lesson on a beautiful afternoon with no one else around. What was really happening was much more frightening.

He drew back the club and swung as hard as he could. The quick click of the ball against the club sounded pure. Better yet was the sight of his ball sizzling through the air, straight as an arrow, toward the marker....not the red marker, or the green, but straight toward the blue one. The crowd gasped as they realized how much farther Zack's ball had gone. It plunked perfectly in the grass a couple of feet in front of the blue marker. A few of the kids even started clapping.

Mr. Barnes walked over to Zack, patted his shoulder, and said, "Well done! That was quite a shot!"

Johnny yelled, "It was just luck. He could never do that twice!"

"He doesn't have to do it twice. He only had to do it once. That's what I said, one shot for each of you," said Mr. Barnes. Zack turned around as he heard some random congratulations from the crowd. "Cool shot." "Sweet!" Those were just a few of the compliments Zack let soak in, knowing this might never happen again.

Johnny yelled, "Let's get out of here. It was a lucky shot! Tub-o couldn't play a real game of golf if his life depended on it."

"What's the matter Johnny…afraid someone might be better than you at *something*?" One of the stooges had questioned Johnny in front of the whole class. Johnny angrily pulled his club from Zack's hand and jammed it into his bag.

Just before he marched off, he glared at Zack. Zack couldn't be sure, but he thought he saw Johnny's eyes welling up with tears before he pouted off to the locker room. *Did I just make Johnny Beam cry?* Was that really the same Johnny Beam that had hit golf balls at him the day before, giving him painful welts and bruises? Zack smiled at the thought.

"All right kids, let's break it up. It's time for everyone to head for lunch." Zack ran out to find his ball. No way would he be leaving the field without the ball that sunk Johnny Beam.

Zack hadn't noticed how fast his heart had been racing until he sat at his desk. He could hear the heavy beating coming from his chest. He let out the deep breath he'd been holding and hoped school would go quickly so he could tell Mr. Vogel.

School seemed to fly by. And it was Friday. On Saturdays, if the weather was nice, he would be at the range from 11:00 am until close.

He walked through the halls keeping his head down as he made his way through the maze of kids. He could hear them talking. They were saying things like, "Did you hear how Big Belly Zack killed Johnny's shot in gym class today?" "I think Johnny was so embarrassed he almost cried!" While Zack grinned on the inside, on the outside he just kept focusing on making it out of school without any trouble.

"Hey, how's that shoulder Zack?" Mr. Vogel questioned.

"Fine," Zack replied.

"Good, because there are a lot of balls to be washed today. Why don't you get started, and I'll be there after awhile." Zack nodded and headed for the washroom. He got a batch of golf balls out of the dryer and dumped a new load into the washer. Zack pulled his box of balls out of his bag and set them on the shelf right next to him. He sunk his hand into his pocket to retrieve the one he had used to reach gossip status at school.

Zack looked out the washroom door just in time to see Johnny standing there with three of his friends. Johnny was looking down at the ball he'd placed on the ground as he drew back his club. Johnny was aiming at the washroom. *He's back for round two!*

Mr. Vogel's voice rang out, "NO WAY! NOT THIS TIME!" Mr. Vogel grabbed Johnny's club right before he took the swing.

"I'm not doing anything, Mister," said Johnny.

"I know better than that. Now get out of here! You and your friends are never allowed back here again. This driving range is closed to you!" Mr. Vogel raised his voice to a level Zack had never heard before.

Johnny reached for his bag. Mr. Vogel snatched it away. "I don't think so! Now scram before I call the police!"

Johnny ran to his bike, which was propped against the fence. Before he took off, he yelled back, "I'm going to get my dad! You'll wish you hadn't taken my clubs!"

"Perfect! Go tell your dad. Then I can tell him what you've been up to," Mr. Vogel shouted back.

Johnny didn't hear him. He had already taken off on his bike. His friends had scattered like frightened mice.

Mr. Vogel turned toward Zack, "Sorry son, these guys will never bother you here again. I don't mind tellin' their parents if they want to get them involved."

"It's all right. Johnny's just mad because I made him look stupid today," Zack let it roll off his tongue almost before he realized what he had said.

"You did what? How?" Mr. Vogel looked a little shocked. He knew for a fact that Zack didn't have the confidence to stand up to Johnny.

"I got a chance in gym class to hit a ball and see if I could hit farther than Johnny. I did it! He made a horrible shot, and my ball went straight as an arrow right toward the blue marker. The kids in my class cheered, and Johnny cried! Well, um, he had tears anyway." Zack was so excited to tell Mr. Vogel that he wasn't sure if he was making any sense as the entire story spilled out all in one breath.

"So you go to school with him?" Mr. Vogel questioned.

"Yeah," Zack admitted. He felt horrible for lying before about not knowing

Johnny. Secretly he hoped Mr. Vogel would let it go so he wouldn't have to explain that he'd been too embarrassed to tell him.

"Congratulations Champ! See, it ain't so bad standin' up to the bully." Mr. Vogel was beaming as he wrapped his arm around Zack's shoulders. "So, this was payback, is that what you're telling me?"

"Yeah, I guess. He was mad." Zack was trying hard not to let what almost happened ruin all the great things that had happened that day.

He considered telling Mr. Vogel about his correct answer during his history lesson, but he thought better of it. In order to tell the story, Mr. Vogel would have to know that Zack had never raised his hand in class before. That victory would have to stay between him and his possibly magic golf balls.

"If today was pay back, what was yesterday?" Mr. Vogel questioned.

"Um, well, uh, yesterday was just Johnny being Johnny." Zack really didn't want to discuss it.

"Well, do you suppose he'll go get his daddy?" Mr. Vogel asked.

"I don't know. I doubt it, because then he'll have to tell him about his day in gym class."

"Yeah, you're right. Then Mr. Beam will realize that all the money he has spent on private golf lessons for his son is money wasted." They both laughed. Mr. Vogel tipped his head back and gave a great big belly laugh. To hear it made Zack laugh harder. It had been a wonderful day.

The two traveled back through Zack's story, filling in the parts that Zack had skipped. While they talked, Zack cleaned the balls, and Mr. Vogel took a short break on a stool next to the washer.

Zack needed to return some equipment to the storage room, and as he turned the corner he could hear a car speeding into the parking lot. Zack had seen this car before. It was Jack Beam, Johnny's dad. His sleek black Lincoln squealed to a stop.

Zack knew little about Mr. Beam. His only encounter with him had been when he had come to school on career day to talk to Zack's class. He had seemed rigid and stuffy in his neatly pressed suit. His hair was black, same as Johnny, and it had been perfectly combed. When he walked into the room it was clear that his presence made other people uncomfortable. Mr. Beam was a big deal real estate developer. He was known for buying all kinds of property and selling it to big commercial companies.

Zack felt nervous as he saw Mr. Vogel standing outside, watching Mr. Beam get out of his car. A cloud of dust stirred up by the speeding car swirled around Mr. Beam's shiny black shoes. Zack wished he could hide, or at least snap his fingers and have Mr. Vogel sucked away, somewhere he'd be free from the wrath of Mr. Beam.

As Mr. Beam stomped up the little hill to where Mr. Vogel was standing, Zack caught sight of Johnny getting out of his dad's car. Two friends accompanied him.

"What in the world is going on in this dump?" Mr. Beam shouted as a greeting.

"Dump? It's only a dump if I allow out of control customers, like your son, to vandalize my property," fired back Mr. Vogel.

"He told me you took his clubs!"

"Absolutely. Johnny and his friends showed up here yesterday hitting golf balls into the washroom where Zack was working. The boys came back today to do it again. It's not going to happen. If Johnny can't use his equipment the way it's meant to be used, then he's not going to use it here."

Before Mr. Vogel could finish, Johnny piped up. "No Dad, we only came here today because Zack tried to hit me with a golf ball in gym class."

"That's not true and you know it," Mr. Vogel stated.

"Yes it is dad! Now this guy won't let us play. I have to practice," whined Johnny.

"I don't know what kind of establishment you're running here Mister, but it would be in your best interest to give my son his equipment back and let him practice. If there is any trouble I could take this place down, and you know it."

"Take it down? What do you mean? You're not taking anything!"

"I've heard about Zack. I've even seen him a time or two. He's the fat, do-nothing kid in Johnny's class. No one like that is going to be pushing my kid around. If you're not careful I'll buy this place, tear it down, and put up condos right here where you stand. Don't test me. Apologize to my son, and give him back his clubs…NOW!"

The temperature outside had suddenly gotten very hot, far beyond comfortable. As the men raised their voices, their faces were getting more red.

"Johnny has been teasing Zack, picking on him every chance he gets, for quite a while now. He's given him a hard time at school, and then he comes here to harass him at work. Zack's a good golfer, and your son is just jealous because there's a good chance that if Zack wanted to be, he could be better than Johnny." Mr. Vogel shouted.

"Now you've gone too far! Johnny's the best junior player this town has ever seen," Mr. Beam countered.

"I have seen him, he's not that good, and Zack is a better player!" Mr. Vogel's voice had gone a step past shouting. Tempers were well beyond boiling.

"If you're so sure that 'Chubby' stands a chance at beating Johnny then let's bet on it!"

"Perfect! What are we betting on?"

"We're betting on your dump here. The city tournament is at the end of the summer. Let's see who wins. You'll have five months to get Zack in shape to *attempt* to beat Johnny. If Johnny wins I own this place….if not, I'll build the best course in the state right here, and Zack will be hailed the best junior player in the city. Zack won't hear another word from Johnny…EVER!" With that, Mr. Vogel threw his hand out to Mr. Beam. Mr. Beam didn't hesitate. They exchanged a strong, anger-filled shake as Mr. Vogel yelled, "You're on!"

You're on? You're on? What does that mean, You're on? Had Mr. Vogel just bet his pride and joy, his precious driving range, on whether or not Zack was a better player than Johnny? His knees began to shake. *There's no way anything good can come out of this.*

As Zack watched Mr. Beam and the boys storm off towards the black Lincoln, Zack sat down. He could hear Mr. Vogel mumbling under his breath as he watched Mr. Beam drive off.

"Get up Zack, we got a little work ahead of us," Mr. Vogel had a slight smile. He had made his comment light heartedly, as if there was nothing to worry about.

"A…a, a little work ahead of us?" Zack stuttered.

"Yeah, I take it you heard all that noise Mr. Beam and I were making?"

"I did…What are we gonna do?"

"Well, we're gonna work hard and win ourselves a tournament. It will be the tournament that gets rid of Johnny Beam and shuts him up for good, son. Don't worry, it'll be great."

"Don't worry? Don't worry!" Zack repeated.

He got up and followed Mr. Vogel as he began to tidy up the counter. Mr. Vogel was acting as though the last few minutes hadn't happened at all.

"Zack, you ought to go home early tonight. You'll need to get some rest; we start training in the morning." Mr. Vogel winked.

Zack hurried to grab his bag. He exited the washroom and headed toward the storage room. He pulled a putter from the stockpile of equipment and carried it home.

Back at home, Zack sat stunned. This had been the biggest day of his entire life. What should he do now? He felt weak when he tried to stand and dizzy when he looked at the putter leaning against the wall.

Zack pulled the furniture out of the way and grabbed a glass from the cupboard. The goal was to get his putt to be just perfect, causing the ball to roll into the glass, tipping it upright. Zack was skeptical that he could do it, but it was worth a try.

He opened his box of balls and placed one on the floor. He putted a few times, completely off target. He grew more and more frustrated each time he tried. *Where is that great aim I had in the field today?*

After several more attempts, Zack picked up the ball and yelled, "What good are you? I thought you were supposed to have some sort of magical power, and I can't even putt with you!" He threw the ball back on the floor, angry that he was losing his temper. He took the balls and his putter and stormed off to his room.

Zack set the glass on the floor. "Just help me out and jump into the cup… please," Zack pleaded. Nothing happened. *I'm gonna have to be better than this if I am gonna have a chance at beating Johnny.* He stared at the ball and concentrated as hard as he ever had. With the next putt, the ball skirted left of the cup. He tried again, and again, and then again. It was hopeless.

"I'm only doin' this *one* more time before I quit and make Mr. Vogel call off this tournament!" Zack yelled into his quiet, lonely bedroom. He put the ball back in place, and with fierce determination, he tried to imagine that he *was* the ball. He tried to picture himself rolling perfectly into the glass. He stood the way Mr. Vogel had taught him, pulled the putter back and whispered, "I just have to *Be the ball.*"

Immediately after saying the words, Zack noticed his ball shaking. He quickly looked over at the box and saw that it too was shaking. The balls began to glow. The light got brighter and brighter until beams of light started shooting out of each ball. Just then the balls darted across the room, banging into the ceiling, knocking into the walls. Golf balls flying around the room, Zack had been here before. He ran for cover, diving under his desk. He closed his eyes tight as crashing sounds filled his ears. Bright light took over Zack's room, forcing him to close his eyes and hide his

face. He squinted, trying to see what was going on. It looked like he was standing in the middle of a rainbow. Every color he had ever seen swirled around his room in a brilliant display. There was nothing he could do but sit and wait. Even though it had only been a minute, to Zack it felt like hours.

The light slowly began to dim, and the crashing stopped. From where he sat, Zack could see six of the balls spread around his room. Out of the corner of his eye, Zack saw something move. He watched as a ball rolled straight toward him and stopped inches from his hiding place. The ball started spinning, faster and faster and faster until in one dramatic movement…four limbs stretched into view. Zack blinked hard.

"Hey there, I'm 'Linx'. Well, 'Dude of the Dozen' if you want to get specific. Some people call me 'Dude,' others call me 'Linx'. I just answer when spoken to. We've been waiting for you! Zackary, Zack, Mr. Z., which do you prefer?" There was a small pause. "Well, don't just sit under there staring at me, get up. Life is better lived in motion, not sitting still. Maybe that's a lesson for another day. First things first there buddy…what should we call you?"

Zack took a big, loud gulp. "Wwwwwe??" Zack stuttered.

"Yes, we. Look around, I've brought my friends."

5

No Quick Fix

Zack's eyes scanned the room. The golf balls that had been sitting motionless were now stretching and dusting themselves off. Zack couldn't think. He just stared.

He blinked hard again. Then he closed his eyes. Right then he heard small, pounding steps above his head, coming from the top of his desk.

"March two, three, and four; pick 'em up two, three, and four. Company… halt!" Zack carefully leaned out from under the desk, just far enough to be able to see where the noise was coming from. Marching in a straight line across the top of his desk was a golf ball wearing a safari helmet. His hands were in fists, and his posture was perfect.

I am dreaming! "Wwwhat's going on?" Zack asked.

The ball stopped, "What do you mean 'what's going on'? And don't you mean, What's going on, 'Sir'?" questioned the ball with a military tone.

"Sorry." Zack said, in almost a whisper. He scrambled to his feet. The ball on his desk was staring back with both hands behind his back.

"Sir, I have a question?" Zack asked.

"What is it boy?"

"What is going on…Sir?"

"Hey, you're getting the hang of it. Nicely done. My friends and I are here on a mission. *Operation Zack*, I believe it's being called. You wouldn't happen to know him, would you boy?"

"That's me. I'm Zack."

The ball looked Zack up and down. He studied Zack's jeans with the big hole in the knee. Next he stared at Zack's un-tucked shirt, the one he had spilled milk on earlier in the day. His eyes then traveled to Zack's light brown, shaggy hair.

"It looks to me like you *could* use a little help. That is, if you want to become a soldier."

"I don't want to become a soldier, Sir," Zack said, still sure he wasn't really having a conversation with a golf ball.

"Hey Zack, don't let Lost get you all confused. He's our 'misguided guide,' if you know what I mean?" Linx said with a wink, as he leaned toward Zack, trying not to let Lost hear him.

"Lost Ball, why don't you scout out some dinner while I get Mr. Z caught up to speed."

"It's Zack."

"Oh, very good. *Zack*, why don't you have a seat?"

Zack sat back on his bed. Linx crawled up and stood right next to him. Just then Zack heard a splash and quickly turned his attention to his nightstand. Bobbing around in his glass of water was a golf ball wearing goggles, a snorkel, and flippers. He began swimming as tiny air bubbles made their way out of his snorkel and surfaced on the top of the water.

"That's Wet. He wasn't meant for dry ground. Wherever there is water to be found, that's where you'll find him. He's a character all right." Linx slapped his knee and laughed a little, obviously thinking about his past experiences with Wet. Zack turned his attention back to the floor where the other balls had been sitting. All of them were gone.

"How many of you are there?" Zack questioned hesitantly.

"Twelve. We're the Magic Dozen. You're in for the time of your life my friend. I assure you."

"Wait…so you're all magic! The note…the box…all of you…you're *alive*! "
In one moment everything that had happened flooded Zack's mind. His thoughts danced from Johnny busting a hole in the wall, to Ben Hogan, to the note; and now, to the fact that he had twelve golf balls roaming around his bedroom. He rubbed his forehead with the palms of his hands as he tried to make sense of it all.

"Don't worry. We're here to help. Consider us the 'penny in your pocket' so to speak. We're professionals. We come when we're called and leave when our work is done. Can't get much better than that, now can you?"

"I guess not. But I still don't get it?"

"Rumor has it you've got a tournament to prepare for…is that correct?"

The tournament! *How could I have forgotten about the tournament? Mr. Vogel will never believe this!*

"Wait, let me get this straight. You guys are all here to help me get ready for the city tournament with Johnny Beam?"

"Well, let's just say, we're here to help with whatever we can, however we can. If that includes the tournament then great, if not then that's all right too. Although, I can't say we're all work and no play," Linx stated as he pointed to three golf balls wearing masks. They were each standing on the other's head so they could get high enough for the top one to throw himself into Zack's garbage can, which was sitting next to his desk.

"That's Triple Bogey. You'll learn to love them."

"Am I going to get to meet all of you?"

"Of course, except some of us are only needed on special occasions. We all play a part, but we're going to save that for tomorrow. You'll need to get some sleep. You've had an exciting day. By the way, congratulations on that correct answer in school. I'll round up the gang. We'll see you tomorrow."

Linx stuck his thumb and middle finger in his mouth and let out a high pitched whistle. He jumped down next to the box on the floor and watched as the other balls filed in.

"How did you know about school?"

"It's called confidence Zack; we all need a little boost sometimes. You did it. We just knew you could."

Zack saw Lost still on top of his desk, digging through his container of paper clips. *Yep, he's lost all right. He couldn't be any farther from finding food...*

Linx whistled one more time, and Lost quickly marched to the edge of the desk and jumped off, landing on the floor, and rolling into the box. Linx counted each ball and then yelled, "Beach, grab your chair and let's go!"

On his nightstand Zack saw small wet footprints that went from his glass, across the surface of his stand, and ended at the edge of the table. Basking in the light of his lamp was Beach, stretched out in a tiny lawn chair; sunglasses on, wearing a straw sun hat.

"Why? Come on Dude, I just got comfortable. Nothin' like a little time in the sun," Beach said.

"It's not the sun Beach, it's a lamp. Now let's go."

"But it's been an eternity since I sat in my chair, soakin' up the rays, enjoyin' life. I'll be right here when you get back. Just let me chill."

"Beach..."

"Simmer down Dude, I'm on my way," Beach mumbled as he slowly got up and folded his chair. He looked up at Zack and waved, "later dude."

"You'll have to excuse him. He calls everyone 'dude' which is why others typically call me Linx. Talk about confusing, huh?"

Suddenly the room was quiet. All the balls had found their places back inside the box. In the blink of an eye, they had returned to normal. Zack bent down and lifted them up. He lifted one ball from its cardboard square and inspected it. Nothing about the ball was out of the ordinary. It looked like every other ball Zack had seen before. Nothing special. The only difference was that they had just proven how deceiving appearances can be.

Zack set the box on his nightstand. He looked at his clock. It was almost 9 o'clock, and he felt exhausted. He heard his stomach grumbling. He took the box of balls with him into the kitchen and heated up a frozen dinner.

Zack put on pajamas, brushed his teeth, and crawled into bed. He was thinking about his talk with Linx when he realized all the furniture in the living room was still out of place. He threw back the covers and ran to clean up his mess. When he got back to bed he reached for his glass. *Maybe I should get a new glass of water.*

Zack woke to water splashing him in the face. He quickly opened his eyes to see Wet floating on his back, spitting a fountain of water out of his mouth.

"Hey, quit that!" yelled Zack.

"Oh, sorry, but this water is wonderful! Did it come from the refrigerator? Filtered? Must be, this is definitely not tap water, and certainly not pond water. It's much better than the swampy water I usually find myself in."

Zack laughed as Wet dove down to the bottom of the glass. It wasn't until Zack turned his attention towards the rest of his bedroom that he saw with his own eyes how challenging his life had just become.

It was chaos. Lost Ball was marching in front of his closet mumbling something about how the others needed to *fall in line*. Triple Bogey had apparently found his colored pencils. They had drawn on top of his desk. It didn't appear to be a picture of anything. His backpack sat on the floor, unzipped. *Triple Bogey must have gone through that too.* A few of the other balls that he had not been introduced to were doing various things around the room. They were mostly just checking things out. A voice from behind him said, "Dude, you wouldn't happen to have any lemonade would ya?" Zack turned to see Beach, again sprawled out in his chair. He had comfortably positioned it on Zack's windowsill, taking in the only ray of sunshine that shone from between the blinds.

"No, I don't. Sorry."

"No worries dude…I just thought that if ya had some…"

Beach was interrupted by Linx. Zack hadn't noticed him before, perched on the post of his headboard.

"How are you this morning Zack?"

"Fine. But I was wondering if you guys would come with me to the driving range?"

"Of course. You'll find it difficult to leave us behind, even if you want to."

"Great. I want you to meet Mr. Vogel. He's going to be so excited to see you. I better hurry and get ready." Zack ran to shower, making certain to leave his bedroom door shut. He didn't want to take any chances that the balls could decide to roam beyond the boundaries of his room. After shoving down a breakfast of his favorite cereal, Sugar Snaps, Zack put on his shoes.

"Linx, could you get everyone together for me so we can go?"

"Absolutely." Linx whistled and again everyone sprang into action. Everyone except one.

"Beach, time to go," ordered Linx.

"Awww man, this is such a drag. I was just getting comfortable. Is there going to be any sand where we're headed?"

"Sorry, not today. We're just going to the driving range. I have someone I want you to meet," said Zack.

"Well, then, I need to tell you…" Linx started.

"There's no time. Sorry Linx. Just jump in with everyone else. We're going to be late," Zack interrupted.

"Well, I think first I should…"

"Whatever it is we can talk about it later, I really don't want to be late."

"All right, suit yourself."

With Linx tucked safely away with the others, Zack grabbed the box and slid it into his bag. He did a quick scan of his room before heading out. Again, water had been tracked onto his nightstand. There were a few pieces of crumpled paper from his wastebasket lying in the middle of the floor. Zack knelt to grab them and throw them away. When he did he could see the container of paper clips that had been spilled off his desk and onto the floor. His closet door had been left open. Clearly one of the balls had been looking for something when they pulled his shirts off the shelf and left them in a heap. They were definitely making an impression.

It wasn't until Zack reached for the knob on the front door that he thought about his mother. How could he forget that she would've come home last night and was probably still sleeping? He set his bag down, ran to his mother's room and softly knocked on the door.

"Mom, are you awake?" Zack whispered.

"Yeah, come in," she answered in her sleepy morning voice.

"Sorry, I'm in a hurry, I just wanted to say 'bye'."

"I'm glad you did. You were sleeping so soundly last night that you didn't even wake up when I came home."

"Ah, yeah, it was a long day with school and the driving range and all, you know."

"Yeah, I thought maybe that was it."

At the range Zack found Mr. Vogel replacing equipment that had been used the day before in the storeroom. He burst through the door. "Mr. Vogel, Mr. Vogel, Mr. Vogel…are you ready for this?" Startled, Mr. Vogel turned to face Zack.

"I didn't expect you to be so excited about your training…but, yes, I am excited. What do you say we get started!?" Zack was temporarily confused. He shook his head and said, "No, no, Mr. Vogel, not the training. It's the balls!"

"The balls? From the box?"

"Yes, they are real…ah, alive, well…*magic!*" As Zack stammered out his answer he began digging in his bag to retrieve the box. Mr. Vogel had a big smile cross his face as he watched Zack. "What's gotten into you?"

"These balls, they can talk! They fly around! Bright lights flash! One got in my water glass!" Zack opened his mouth and let the news fall right out. Now all there was left to do was try to explain.

"They don't just talk, they also walk…well, and swim…and they're smart. See, I'll show you." Mr. Vogel watched Zack carefully as he set the box containing the balls on the countertop underneath the window. A beam of light was shining through, and happened to be illuminating the very spot Zack had chose to set the balls.

This simple glowing light made Zack think back to when the balls first came alive. The display had been amazing. Until now he had not thought back to the lights and firework show he had seen when he first said, *"Be the ball."* That was something he would have to remember to ask Linx about. Would Mr. Vogel get the same display? If that was the case, maybe Mr. Vogel should be sitting.

"All right. Here, sit down," Zack offered as he pulled a wooden stool up next to the counter. "I was at home putting last night. I got really mad because I kept missing, and I said something and…well, and the balls came alive. There was light, bright light, and the balls were flying around my room, and then I met Linx…"

"Whoa, slow down there boy. I'm going to ask again. What has gotten into you?" Mr. Vogel was smiling an uncomfortable smile as he shook his head.

"Nothing, it's the balls. They say they're here to help. "

"Are you tellin' me that you think they're real?"

"Yes," Zack replied confidently. Mr. Vogel's expression didn't change. After a moment, he reached over and lifted the lid off the box.

"Good idea, I'll just show you instead of tell you," said Zack.

Mr. Vogel had picked up one of the balls and was turning it over in his hand. "Yeah, you better, because right now all I see is a golf ball. Actually, I see 12 golf balls, and they all appear to be the same ones you left with last night, and the night before that."

"I know. They can do that when they want to. But, if you want them to wake up, there is something you've got to say."

"What exactly was it you said when they, um, *came alive?*" asked Mr. Vogel.

Zack leaned over to Mr. Vogel and whispered, "All you have to say is, '*Be the ball.*'"

"And then there will be flashing lights, and they start flying around, talking, walking, and swimming? Have I got this right?" asked Mr. Vogel.

"Just try it!" Zack was feeling impatient. More than anything he wanted to see the look on Mr. Vogel's face when he saw that everything Zack had said was true.

"Here I go. '*Be…the…ball.*'" Nothing happened. Mr. Vogel looked at Zack. "Do you see anything, because I don't? Did I do it right?"

Zack pulled Linx from his cardboard square and held him close to his face. "Didn't you hear Mr. Vogel? He said, '*Be the ball.*'" Zack overemphasized the phrase, hoping Linx just hadn't heard it the first time. Again, nothing.

"Hey guys quit playing around and get up." Zack pleaded with Linx as Mr. Vogel began inspecting the other balls.

Just then Linx stretched out his arms and legs. "Here he is! Look! Mr. Vogel! Quick!"

"Now do you have time to listen to me, Zack?" Linx questioned.

"Son, I don't know what is going on, but all I see is a box of golf balls. If you'd like to pretend that these are magical balls, just let me know. I'll play along if it means we can get started on your training," suggested Mr. Vogel.

"Don't you see him? This is Linx, he's the leader of the pack." As Zack said it he held Linx out in the palm of his hand.

"So you've named him, that's nice Zack." It was clear by the tone in his voice and the expression on his face that Mr. Vogel and Zack were not seeing the same thing.

"Are you ready now?" Linx asked. Zack just shook his head. "He can't see us, Zack. Nobody can. It's just you and us…that's all. To you I am moving and talking. To him, I am sitting perfectly still in the last place I was left. We are here for you."

Zack's shoulders fell. *Wish I would've known that a little sooner. Now what am I going to do? Mr. Vogel might as well hand over his driving range right now and save everyone all the trouble. He's going to lose everything to Mr. Beam anyway.*

If Mr. Vogel had any confidence in Zack before, it had probably just been shot to the ground. He would think Zack was crazy for sure. There was really no way out of this.

On the range, one blue, one red, and one green marker were set up. Mr. Vogel set down the clubs and said, "Now you said the balls are here to help. Is that correct?"

"Yeah."

"Well now, don't look so upset. I'm not saying it couldn't happen. I just can't see it. Grab a ball and let's see if they're any good," Mr. Vogel's friendly, contagious smile returned.

"You see that green flag about 150 yards to your left? Let's see you get within 15 feet of it…with the help of…Linx did you say?"

When Zack turned to pick a club he looked at Linx and very quietly whispered, "Are you even going to be able to help me?"

"I could help you, but this looks like a job better suited for Long Ball. Have you two had a chance to meet?" asked Linx.

"No, but at this point I'll try anything."

"Good, just set me back and grab the ball to my right. He never misses a chance to go flying."

Zack did exactly as Linx asked. He placed Long Ball on the grass, wondering if disappointment awaited him after he swung his club. He lined himself up, took aim, and hit. Unbelievably the ball lifted off his club and went airborne directly toward the green flag. Long Ball dropped into the grass about five feet in front of the marker, bounced once, and finished perfectly in the hole supporting the green flag.

Zack didn't know what to do. He just stood there with his mouth open. No one said a word. Zack shook his head and walked in the direction of the green flag. Just before he got there he saw Long Ball jump out of the hole.

"Nice shot, don't you think? Could've done without that bounce though. Feels good to be back in the game," Long Ball said as he gently rubbed his head. Zack picked him up, smiled, and whispered, "*thank you.*" When Zack got back to Mr. Vogel, he found him still standing there, supported by his 4 iron, staring towards the green flag.

"Now do you believe me?" Zack asked.

"Zack, if you can learn to hit like that consistently, I wouldn't care if you told me we were living on Mars, I'd believe you."

It wasn't exactly the answer Zack was looking for, but it made him laugh. As long as Mr. Vogel wasn't going to press him for an explanation about all the strange things he had told him earlier, Zack was happy.

"Let's get started. I've set up some training exercises for you today. The most important thing to remember is that this will be a process. There will be no 'quick fixes' on the road to becoming great at anything, no matter what it is. The only way you are going to become a tournament player is by learning the game, focused dedication, and a lot of hard work. Natural talent will only take you so far. You have to decide how bad you want this. Let's start by having you tell me about it."

Mr. Vogel's face had begun to change during his speech. Zack could see a new glimmer in his eye. Along with the excitement that was present, Zack saw something entirely different. He had never seen Mr. Vogel so intense about anything. His naturally laid back personality had masked the determined spirit that brewed within him. The new challenge had seemed to awaken the Mr. Vogel who was accustomed to working hard, getting down to business, and striving to become the best. *This must be how Mr. Vogel was during the tour.*

Zack began to think about how much work he had ahead of him. How many hours had Mr. Vogel practiced to become as good as he was? A fire Zack had never felt before began to rise within his spirit. He felt the energy coming from Mr. Vogel, and he grew more aware of what this tournament really meant. Zack drew in a large breath and let all his desires roll off his tongue in one steady stream.

"I do want this. I want to beat Johnny. I want Mr. Beam to build you the best golf course this city has ever seen. I want everyone to know that Johnny cheats, and lies, and that he's mean...I want to work really hard so I don't ever have to be afraid of Johnny again. I want my days of being teased and picked on to be done! I want to have friends at school. I want to see Johnny cry again. I want to be the best junior player in town. *I really want this!*"

When Zack was finished, he had a lump in his throat that he was having trouble fighting to keep down. He swallowed hard to try and resist all the feelings that had welled up inside of him. He finally let it sink in that everything in his life, and Mr. Vogel's, was riding on whether or not he could beat Johnny.

Calmly Mr. Vogel said, "Good. That's what I wanted to hear. And that's what I want to see. Determination. There is nothing like the feeling of accomplishing your goals. However, with that said, there is something else you need to remember. You will not wake up every day feeling like you are feeling right now. You are in the exciting beginning phase. This will pass. When it feels like it's getting too hard, remember this…remember everything you just told me. Remember *how* you told me. When you're tired and don't feel like working anymore…just remember."

6

"What Do You See?"

Mr. Vogel reached into his back pocket and took out a blindfold.

"What is that for?" Zack questioned.

"This is going to be your friend for the day. In the game of golf, the mental side of the sport is more important than the physical side. Both are important in their own way, but right now we are going to focus on the mental part. I am going to teach you *how* to see." He turned Zack around and placed the blindfold over his eyes. Next, he squared his shoulders to the tee. "What do you see Zack?"

"Um, nothing."

"Come on now, what do you *see*?" Mr. Vogel asked again.

Zack was confused. *Surely Mr. Vogel knows he just blind folded me. There's nothing to see here.*

"There is only darkness, just like any other time I close my eyes."

"Can't you see that big golf course laid out in front of you? See the hills and all that the course has to offer? There, that breeze…what direction is it coming from?"

Zack started visualizing everything Mr. Vogel was saying. Soon the most amazing golf course in the world was rolled out at his feet. The grass was the most vibrant shade of green. There was a slight breeze, just enough to cool Zack off and settle his nerves. He could see the rolling hills and clusters of trees. There was even a small pond off to his right.

Moments later Zack felt Mr. Vogel place a club in his hands. After Zack had a firm grip, Mr. Vogel directed the club to the ball. "Now swing. But don't just give it any swing. Watch as the ball flies off the grass and soars toward the green, gently landing near the pin. You need to visualize the perfect shot *every* time. Now go, swing."

Zack lined up his club, drew back, and gave the best swing he could. In his mind's eye Zack could see the ball flying through the air. Perfect.

Mr. Vogel told Zack to continue swinging until he returned. After about 100 swings, Zack's hands and shoulders were getting tired. He hoped Mr. Vogel would be back soon.

"Mr. Vogel, are you here?" Zack called out. There was no response. He was thankful for a little more time because he had not heard from Linx in awhile.

"Linx, are you here?"

"Staring right at you champ." Linx replied.

"…And staring at his picture of sweet little Miss *Teena,* too!" Yelled one of the balls. With that comment came a flood of laughter.

"So I guess everyone is still here then," replied Zack.

"Just ignore Beach, he doesn't know what he's talking about."

"Don't know what I'm talkin' about? We all know what I'm talkin' about. We see you sneak little glances at that picture you keep in your pocket *all the time*! You miss her, we know you do! Don't be ashamed there Dude, she's a heartbreaker."

"Focus on the task at hand, Beach. Yes, Zack, we are all here. Everyone's amazed at your teacher. Why are we here to help when you've got him? Well, there must be a reason! There is always a reason! How are you feeling?" inquired Linx.

"Tired. And I'm not sure how good I can get when I'm blindfolded. He's really making me work."

"Looks like it, although I don't think he'll be the only one."

Just then Zack could hear footsteps approaching. He gave one more air swing and then stopped. "Mr. Vogel, is that you?"

"Yeah. Who were you talking to?"

"Nobody. Just myself I guess."

"Were you discussing the game, and how your swing is improving, making you the best junior player this town has ever seen?" Mr. Vogel asked seriously.

Zack smiled. "Can I take this blindfold off now?"

"Five more swings, and then we'll talk about it. Concentrate and focus!" directed Mr. Vogel.

After his final swing Zack took off the blindfold.

"These are yardage markers. I have marked every 25 yards. As you can see, there are four of them. I want you to select the right club for each shot. You will have to hit 100 balls at each marker. I will show you how to hit using a three-quarter swing and then a one-half swing," instructed Mr. Vogel.

"A hundred balls at each marker! Do I have to hit 100 balls using a three-quarter swing and a one-half swing at every marker?!"

"Yes. And then we'll move on to our next exercise."

"I can't hit," started Zack, but Mr. Vogel was already interrupting him.

"What did you just say? We have only been out here a half hour, and already you're telling me you *can't*? That stops here. If you expect greatness, then there is no room for 'I can't'. Deal?"

"Deal," Zack mumbled.

"Well, I'd say this guy's a bit of slave driver, wouldn't you?" Zack immediately recognized the voice of Lost Ball. He looked over to where he had left the box of balls on the ground earlier. All of them were standing, staring directly at Zack.

"Hi, guys. Yeah, Mr. Vogel's turning into a tough one."

"That's all right, it's good for you. He's strong; I like him," said Lost Ball.

"Yeah dude, you totally would," proclaimed Beach from his sun chair.

"It's too bad you need this harsh kind of training. Now, if you were just a little more like me."

"What's your name?" Zack questioned.

"I'm You Da Man…you know, because I *am Da Man*." He said as he used both thumbs to point to himself.

"All right everyone, I think now is a good time to introduce each one of you to our newest friend, Zack," stated Linx.

"I wanna meet ya, but we have to be quick. If Mr. Vogel sees that I'm not practicing, he's not gonna be very happy. And it looks like it's gonna rain."

"Perfect, my thoughts exactly," said Linx, looking up at the sky. "Come on guys, let's make a straight line so that Zack can get a good look at you."

"He already knows me. So I think I'll just hang over here until someone needs me dudes. Don't worry Zack; I've got your back too. Ya know where to find me," said Beach.

"Let's start with Mulligan. He's originally from Scotland. You'll find him to be a wonderful support. He believes in always getting a second chance, no matter what has happened." Zack looked at Mulligan who was wearing a very cool plaid hat.

"Nice to see you laddie," Mulligan replied in a definite Scottish accent.

"It's clear you've just met You Da Man. He is who he is, and he is always good to have around when you need an extra boost of confidence. If you know what I mean. You've already met Lost Ball, who will be here to help you, no matter what you need, and will continue to do so, as long as it's not for directions."

"Hey, watch it. I have been thoroughly trained; I can find anything, anytime, anywhere, even in a storm," objected Lost.

"Right, okay, moving on…next we have Wet. He is wonderfully skilled in the art of environmental sciences. He loves the water, and as you have discovered, he will find it no matter where it is."

"Hello. My love is for the earth and all of its beauty, however, most of that beauty is found underneath the water. I'll help, you'll see," said Wet.

Zack felt a drop of rain although the sun was still shining. He looked around the range for Mr. Vogel. He was nowhere to be seen. Zack turned his attention to the line of balls.

The next golf ball in line was wearing a top hat and a mask that looked like a bird's beak. Before Linx even introduced him, he began a little song and dance number. More clouds had moved in, and the rain drops seemed to be coming down a little faster. "Singin' in the rain, just singin' in the rain…what a glorious feeling I'm happy again," Birdie finished singing and started whistling.

"This is Birdie. He never misses a chance to perform. He's quite the ham. He will sing your ear off if you're not careful, and can dance the shoes right off his feet."

At that introduction Birdie stopped in his tracks to take a deep bow. Zack tried to muffle his laugh.

"Here is Greenie, one of our best," continued Linx.

"Good to meet you. Hopefully you'll be sending me onto those greens after you learn to swing a little better. We could be a fierce team, you and me," said Greenie.

"This is Triple Bogey. And I believe you've met them."

Linx pointed to Zack's towel that had previously been draped over one of the clubs in his golf bag. Now it was on the ground, moving away from the bag. Zack reached over and picked up the towel. Underneath he found three balls, all wearing masks. Zack remembered seeing them climbing into his wastebasket the night before. All three turned and looked up at Zack.

"Hi!"

"Hi!"

"Hi!"

"Hi, nice to meet you. Are you gonna cause trouble all the time?" Zack asked.

"We don't cause trouble, we help."

Based on what he had seen, Zack doubted that.

"There you have it. That's everybody. If there's nothing else, then we are going to stay out of your way while you continue to practice," Linx said.

"Hold on there just a minute. What about me?" Long Ball was sitting on the tee, ready to be rocketed off. "I've helped you once. I'm Long Ball. Now what do you say we get this show on the road and you send me flying, right out there to that marker."

"Long Ball, you know the rules. We can't help him all the time. For now he needs to strengthen his game and work with Mr. Vogel. Get off that tee," ordered Linx.

"Oh, come on, just one more time. Send me right over there, and then I'll leave you alone."

Zack couldn't resist one more shot, even though it was really starting to rain now. He lined himself up and gave Long Ball the best swing he had in him. The shot was good, and Long Ball landed exactly where Zack had been aiming.

Back at the washroom, Zack put the box of balls back in his bag, tucked his bag in his locker, and grabbed a towel to dry his face. Zack suddenly realized how hungry he was.

Next door to the driving range was one of Zack's favorite fast food restaurants. It cooked the kind of greasy burgers and fries that no one in town could get enough of. They also made an amazing chocolate shake, fully equipped with whipped cream and a cherry on top. Zack went in and ordered his usual.

After lunch, it had stopped raining. Zack grabbed the Magic Dozen, picked up his golf bag, and trudged back out to the driving range. Mr. Vogel was already waiting. On the grass sitting next to the tee was a small ramp. Zack had never seen anything like it before.

"What is this?"

"This is a ramp. It's going to help you learn how to hit a ball when it lands on the uphill or the downhill slope. You need to know how to hit every shot. This will help," said Mr. Vogel.

Mr. Vogel spent some time showing Zack the different lies a ball could take and the preparation needed for making the next shot. The two of them worked together through the slow afternoon. Only a few customers came in as the day grew warmer. Mr. Vogel took another half hour working on Zack's swing. To wrap up the lessons for the day, Mr. Vogel brought out the blindfold again, and Zack practiced a little longer.

On his way home Zack could feel movement in his backpack. He stopped, opened his bag, and saw that every ball was out of place.

"What are you guys doing?"

"We're just tired of being stuck in this here box, dude," Beach replied.

"Hey, are we heading back to your house? There's still lots more to see and do there," Triple Bogey yelled in unison.

Zack picked up his half-opened bag and put it on backwards so he could see the Magic Dozen. Before he had a chance to answer Triple Bogey, Zack saw Lost Ball. He had climbed up to the top of the bag. He was looking out, shielding his eyes from the sun, and squinting to see as far as he could. "No, we're not headin' home. We've never been this way before."

"Yes you have. This is the way home," corrected Zack.

"Well, we might be headin' home, but it's not the same way we went this morning," Lost insisted. Zack rolled his eyes, remembering what Linx had said about Lost Ball. It was true; he was slightly *misguided*.

Inside the apartment, Zack found a note from his mom. "Sorry buddy, got called in to work. As always, dinner is in the freezer. Call if you need anything. Don't wait up. Love, Mom." Zack was a little disappointed, but too tired to care.

After heating up his dinner, he grabbed a soda and headed to his room. He sat on his bed and kicked off his shoes.

"Hey, what do you think you're doing?" Linx asked.

"Almost done eating, what are you doing?"

"I am watching what you're eating. That's going to have to change you know. You worked hard today. If you want to be the best, you have to be careful about what you put into your body. It's a bigger deal than you realize. If you want to have the stamina to work hard, you have to fuel your body. This junk is not helping. You need a big glass of water. You need *real* food, like fruit and vegetables. You need stuff that is going to help your body perform," instructed Linx.

"This is good food. I guess I could drink some water, but I don't think there are any fruits or vegetables here."

"Let's go to the kitchen. Lead the way, Zack. These guys will be fine until we get back. The first stop will be to dump that soda down the drain," said Linx.

"No way! I love this soda. Just let me finish this one, and next time I will drink water."

"Zack, remember everything Mr. Vogel said. If you're going to get serious, you are going to have to make better choices."

Linx knocked the soda off the counter and into the sink. Zack let out a loud sigh as he watched his soda run down the drain. He knew what Linx was going to say next, so he grabbed a glass and filled it with water. The water tasted fine, and definitely cured his thirst. It just wasn't as good as soda.

Zack could see Linx scanning the countertop. "There, over there in the fruit basket." Zack walked over and lifted up a brown, mushy banana. "You don't expect me to eat *this* do you?"

"Well, no, I guess not. Let's check the refrigerator." Zack opened each drawer. Both the vegetable and fruit trays were empty. What they found was pudding snacks and pizza. A large plastic container held a brownie dessert. On the bottom shelf Linx spotted three cups of yogurt.

"Hey look. Yogurt is good for you. Which do you prefer, peach or blueberry?" asked Linx.

By 8:30 p.m., Zack could not keep his eyes open any longer. Just before he turned off the light, he remembered there was a very important question he had to ask Linx. He turned over to look at the nightstand.

"Wait, before you get back in the box there is something I have to know."

"Anything, what is it?" said Linx.

"Did you really know Ben Hogan? Did you hang out with him, like you are with me? You have to tell me because he's the greatest!"

"He's the greatest what? Maybe he focused and practiced really hard, just like you? Maybe he became great by discipline and desire. That wouldn't make you two all that different, would it?"

"Okay, okay, but I need to know," repeated Zack.

"I think you've learned enough tonight. It's time to get some sleep. The morning is going to come early." Linx jumped back into the box on Zack's nightstand with the others. As his head fell back against his pillow, he wondered what Linx was talking about. Why was morning going to come early? It would be Sunday.

7

"Call 911"

Zack felt tapping on his forehead. He jumped. After rubbing the sleep from his eyes, he looked over at the box. Sure enough not one ball was there. Right away he noticed how sore his shoulders and back felt. All he wanted to do was stay in bed.

"Good morning Zack, we're ready to go; time to get up." It was Linx, standing on Zack's pillow, looking well rested. *It's still dark outside…what's the deal?* The sky had only recently begun to lighten. The clock by his bed read 5:30 a.m.

"What are you doing? Can't you tell time? It's way too early! Everyone needs to go back to sleep," grumbled Zack.

"Go back to sleep? We have to take advantage of this day. There is no school, and you're not due at the driving range until this afternoon. Get up! Get up! You've got some jogging to do," commanded Linx.

"Jogging? No one said anything about jogging. What does that have to do with winning this tournament? Sleep, that's what I need," insisted Zack.

"Up, up, up! Your mind and body need to be at the peak of performance. It's time to eat another cup of yogurt and get the blood flowing through that body. Jogging will help you trim up and stay healthy, all part of the plan!"

With a groan Zack climbed out of bed and shuffled to the kitchen with Linx on his shoulder. They had another discussion about Zack's food choices when Zack had reached for the box of sugar cereal instead of taking yogurt out of the refrigerator. Linx won in the end.

As Zack sat down to eat, Linx mumbled under his breath, "I'm starting to understand why we're here…"

"What does that mean?" Zack asked.

"Nothing," said Linx.

"I can't believe I have to run with my backpack on! You guys are heavy." Zack was thankful that at Linx's urging he'd grabbed a water bottle from the refrigerator.

"Ah, this is great fun Laddie," said Mulligan. "Besides, if this gets too hard, you can take us all home and try it again!"

"That's it, keep up the good work. I could run faster though. Let me down, I'll show you," said You Da Man.

Zack picked up the pace in an attempt to hush the nagging ball. When Zack reached the track at school he stopped. Setting down his bag, he walked around in circles trying to slow his pounding heart and catch his breath.

"Come on my boy, what are ya doin'?" Now it was Lost Ball's turn to chime in.

"Guys… I'm…exhausted! I can't do this…" Zack sputtered between gasping breaths.

"You just think you can't. You can do it. Let's see that determination you used yesterday when you were talking to Mr. Vogel. This is the time he said you'd not *feel* like working hard. Push through it. Let's go!" cheered Linx.

Zack grabbed the bag and ran as hard as he ever had. He could feel the sweat running down his back. Soon it was running down his face and neck. He had never worked this hard. Twice he stopped for long gulps of water.

"Good work, now let's slow it down. Time to walk it out. Take the track once more and then head for home. That was great work for your first day," praised Linx.

The balls seemed to know just what Zack needed to do and weren't afraid to push him. Through his pain, Zack smiled. Life had definitely changed in just a few short days.

Zack had a shower and then quickly ate a piece of cold pizza before Linx could tell him not to. Pizza was, after all, the healthiest of his options. Linx had coached Zack through breakfast about telling his mom what things he'd like to see come off the grocery list, and which ones should be added. It wasn't going to be easy.

At 1 o'clock Zack grabbed the balls and headed for the range. Mr. Vogel had asked him to come over and swing some more. He knew Zack's shoulders would be sore and suggested he come loosen them up.

Mr. Vogel and Zack practiced for a few hours. Zack didn't see or feel much improvement, just blisters on his hands.

"How come I'm not getting any better?" Zack questioned.

"This is only day two, son. Practice takes time. The key is to never give up. You won't see results for awhile. It'll happen, don't worry." But Zack wasn't convinced.

Just before it was time for Zack to go home, he found Triple Bogey in the washroom. They had climbed up on a shelf and knocked over a box of tees. They were throwing them off the shelf. The washer seemed to be their target.

After Zack said good bye to Mr. Vogel, Linx informed him that Wet was not in the backpack.

"Where could he be?"

"I don't know, Zack. When was the last time you were near water?"

Immediately Zack knew where to find Wet. He ran back into the washroom to see him floating on his back in the washer. He reached in and scooped him up.

At home that night Zack finally had some time with his mom. They watched a movie and ate popcorn. Zack was sure Linx would have something to say about that. He used the time to talk about her next trip to the store. She seemed a little confused by his sudden desire to eat salad and fruit. But she agreed that having some healthier choices could do both of them some good.

The next morning Zack still couldn't decide what to do with the balls when he went to school. Sunday had been proof enough that if he brought them with him, he would risk losing them, or having them make trouble that he wouldn't be able to explain. After getting ready and eating breakfast, Zack broke the news to the balls.

"Guys, I have to leave you here today. I'll be back soon. Hang out in my room, ok?" All of the balls started talking and objecting at once.

"I'm sorry. You can't come. I won't be long. Promise. Someday I'll bring you, just not today." The only one who didn't mind was Beach. He had listened to the conversation from his usual spot on the window sill.

On his way to school Zack wondered how bad Johnny would be today. He hadn't been face to face with Johnny since he had made him cry on Friday. This is definitely going to be bad.

During an English lesson Zack noticed his backpack move slightly. He felt a knot in his stomach. *Weren't the balls in my room when I left?* Slowly he picked his bag up off the floor and unzipped it.

"Thank you Zack, it was getting stuffy in here," Birdie said. Then he jumped out and stood on Zack's desk. Right behind him, Zack caught Triple Bogey trying to climb out. Birdie began with a little tap dance. Quickly he scooped up Birdie, put him back in his bag, and zipped it tightly. *How did they get into my bag? Now what am I gonna do?*

English finally finished and there was a short break for recess. With his backpack securely strapped to his back he headed outside.

In the hallway Zack felt something wrap around the front of his ankle. In an instant his face was an inch from the floor. He had tried to catch himself, but it had happened too fast. Everyone laughed. The loudest laugh, raising high above all the others was coming from Johnny Beam. Zack came to his knees just in time to hear Johnny yell as he walked past, "Feet feeling a little *heavy* today Zack? Just like the rest of you!" There was another explosion of laughter.

During recess Zack walked out by the track to be alone. He opened his bag and heard all of the balls talking.

"Who was that kid?"

"Don't worry, we're on it!" yelled Triple Bogey.

"That's the kid Zack is going to beat in the golf tournament," said Linx.

All together the balls seemed to understand. In unison they chimed, "Ohhhh, and nodded at each other."

Zack zipped his bag back up. He didn't want to talk to anyone. His knees hurt from hitting the floor. His shoulders were sore from the last two days, and, above all else, he was embarrassed.

After the bell rang, all the kids filed back into the hallway. Zack saw Johnny at the water fountain getting a drink. As he got closer he saw something in the fountain. It was Wet! *Oh no, what am I going to do?* Zack's mind was reeling.

Zack walked closer to the fountain. Just then there was a huge spray of water, hitting Johnny right in the face. He jumped back, spitting and wiping his eyes. Zack didn't know what happened. When he looked back at the fountain he saw Wet wedged into the stream of water on the spout. He was laughing and splashing around. Zack quickly grabbed Wet as he felt Johnny tap him on the shoulder.

"What do you think you're doing Tubby?"

"Nothing, I...I didn't do anything."

"I saw you. You sprayed me in the face with water! Everyone saw you!" Johnny was pointing at him and everyone was staring. Mrs. Korey came around the corner.

"What's going on?"

"I didn't do it, I wasn't even touching the fountain," Zack pleaded.

"Boys, get back into class, stop fighting. Johnny, you'll dry," said Mrs. Korey.

Class started with a lesson in language arts. "Zack, why don't you take out your book and read the first paragraph for the class."

Zack froze. He didn't know what to do. He had only read out loud one time in class. He had done a terrible job, and never wanted to do it again. With his book open on his desk, he began to stutter through the first sentence. Then he came to a word that no matter how hard he tried, he just couldn't pronounce.

"R..rrr..ri..re.."

Linx jumped up onto his desk and looked at his book. "The word is 'rival', Zack."

Linx continued to help him through the paragraph. By the time it was over Zack was sweating. Johnny made a comment about Zack being stupid when Mrs. Korey turned her back to write on the white board. Everyone laughed.

A few minutes later Zack broke the lead on his pencil, forcing him to get up in front of the class to use the sharpener. When he walked past Johnny's desk, Johnny stuck his foot out. Again, Zack found himself face down on the floor. Slowly he stood, sharpened his pencil, and sat back down. The kids were still laughing.

Zack noticed Triple Bogey walking down the aisle. He tried calling to them to get back in his bag. Johnny heard him talking and turned around. "Don't make me come back there, Zack!" Johnny threatened quietly.

Johnny raised his hand and asked if he could go to the bathroom. No doubt it was so he could have an excuse to walk past Zack. He stood up to leave. Before his feet ever came out from under his desk, Johnny found *himself* on the ground. The class roared. Zack smiled. He didn't know what had happened, but he liked it. Triple Bogey appeared from under Johnny's desk giving each other high fives. Johnny jumped up to find his shoe laces tied together. "Mrs. Korey, Zack did it! When he fell he must have tied my laces together!" Mrs. Korey looked at Zack, who just shrugged and shook his head no.

"Get up and go to the bathroom and hurry back," ordered Mrs. Korey.

"Zack, you can run now, or we can go jogging after you practice at the driving range," suggested Linx. Zack decided to run to the range and get the jogging over with. He ran with the encouragement of Linx whispering in his ear the whole time. He arrived at the driving range tired and sweating. Mr. Vogel had practice all lined up for him. It was another tiring day.

At home Zack and Linx found fruit in the basket on the counter and salad in the refrigerator. There was also more yogurt, eggs, and skim milk. In the cupboard they found whole wheat bread, raisins, and a can of mixed nuts. "None of this stuff looks very good. I can see why my mom never bought it for me before."

"I'd say your mom gets an A+ for her effort. This is great. You'll thank me later. Now, let's make dinner." While Zack ate, Linx went off to rally the Magic Dozen.

"I need everyone's attention. Did anyone else notice how much trouble Zack had reading today?" All the balls agreed that it had been a struggle. "I am going to need everyone's help. We have to do *something* to get him excited about his school work. He needs to be a champion all the way around. We start tonight."

Each night for the next three weeks, the balls gathered around Zack's desk to hear him read out loud. Zack hated it, but he had gotten a little better. Mulligan's strength was math. Wet had helped with science, and Linx and Long Ball helped with vocabulary tests.

Thankfully, that was not the only thing that had improved. There had only been a small amount of teasing from Johnny Beam since he had accused Zack of spraying him with water and tying his shoe laces together.

Zack noticed how much better he was feeling. Every morning Zack was waking up before school to go running, and then making it home to shower and get to school. Last weekend Zack had started to notice how much farther he could run. And, to top it off, the balls had been behaving for the most part.

Zack was still not loving the salads Linx made him eat. But, he knew a major change was taking place. When he was practicing at the driving range with Mr. Vogel he was craving a large glass of orange juice, instead of his usual soda.

Saturday morning came and Zack showed up at the driving range. Mr. Vogel was in his car. "Jump in son, today we're gonna have a change of scenery."

"Where are we going? Who's going to stay at the range?" asked Zack.

"Don't worry about any of that, I took care of it. We're off to the beach!" Zack was ecstatic. He loved the beach, but rarely got to go. *Mr. Vogel must be rewarding me for all my hard work.*

As they got out of the car Zack grabbed his backpack. He hadn't noticed Mr. Vogel rummaging around in the trunk, or the fact that he had grabbed a bag of golf clubs before leaving the range.

The two walked by the water. Zack took off his shoes and socks. There was nothing better than feeling wet sand between his toes. Zack took the Magic Dozen out of his backpack and set them down on the ground. He laughed to himself when he thought about what Wet and Beach were going to do.

"Zack, close your eyes," said Mr. Vogel.

Zack did, half expecting this to be another exercise.

"Now hold out your hands."

Again, Zack did as he was told. Suddenly he felt something really heavy. A strap was laid across his hands.

"Open your eyes." Mr. Vogel said.

"Mr. Vogel, I don't understand. Where did you get these?"

"They're for you."

"But…how can…why? These are the best. They're Ben Hogan clubs!" Zack stammered. Mr. Vogel laughed.

"You've been practicing long enough with rental clubs. It's time you got a set of your own. Every pro needs good equipment. You've proven your dedication. I'm proud of you. So what do you say you try them out?"

"I don't know what to say…I …I love them. They're so cool! Thank you." Zack pulled the clubs out one at a time, admiring how the sun gleamed off the spotless metal. They were awesome. No one had ever given him anything so great in his whole life.

The rest of the day was spent learning how to hit golf balls out of the sand. It was hard, but Zack focused on his game with renewed energy. Not only did he posses the Magic Dozen, he was also playing with his very own set of Ben Hogan clubs. Life had been looking up for Zack.

It appeared life was just as good for Wet and Beach, at least on this particular day. Every time Zack heard Wet splashing around, or Beach asking for lemonade, he laughed. The time flew by. Too soon they had to make the long drive back.

It was 3 o'clock by the time they returned to the range. "You've worked hard today. Hitting out of the sand isn't easy. We have one more exercise to do, and then we'll wrap it up," Mr. Vogel informed Zack. They walked out to the practice green.

Mr. Vogel took out something that looked like a pair of knitting needles tied together with an elastic band. He stretched it out and stuck one end in the ground about six inches behind the hole. The other end was placed about 12 feet from the cup.

"Now, this is going to help you learn to putt from this distance. Remember to make sure that if your ball doesn't make it in the cup, it needs to go past it. The ball can't go in if you don't get it there. No chance of any putt getting in the hole if you leave your ball short," explained Mr. Vogel.

Zack had been practicing his putting for about an hour when he saw a baseball come flying onto the green. It landed about 15 feet to Zack's left side. He looked around but didn't see anyone. He went over to the ball, but Linx had already gotten there.

"How's the training been going?" Zack overheard Linx ask. "Where are you practicing?" Silence. "Really? Sounds fun." Just then Linx turned around.

"Hey Zack, sorry, I didn't see you there."

"Who were you just talking to?"

"Um, well, no one really. What do you say we get back to your practice?"

"I heard you talking. Who were you talking to?"

"There's no one, really. Now let's go," said Linx.

"Where did this baseball come from?" Zack asked.

"I think it came from that little park beyond those trees," said Linx.

Zack picked it up and rolled it around in his hands. He inspected it; sure that something was not quite right. It was a clean, almost new white baseball.

Zack took the baseball, picked up Linx, and walked to the other side of the trees. There he found a boy with a bat. He was small with dark hair and tan skin. Zack noticed how skinny he was. The boy seemed slightly out of place as he tried to handle his bat and swing at another ball.

"Does this belong to you?" Zack asked.

"Yeah, thanks. I've *never* hit *that* far before."

Zack tossed the ball over the fence to the boy and headed back to the green.

Another half hour passed before Mr. Vogel came back. Zack putted the ball into the cup three out of five times. He was happy, and Mr. Vogel seemed pleased.

As Mr. Vogel knelt to pick up his knitting needle contraption, Zack heard a deep thud and turned around in time to see Mr. Vogel fall on his side. Zack ran to him and yelled, "Mr. Vogel, are you okay? What's going on? Are you hurt?"

Mr. Vogel said nothing. His eyes were closed. His hat had been knocked off, and Zack could see a very large bruise starting to form on Mr. Vogel's left temple. Zack jumped up and yelled, "Quick! Someone! Anyone…call 911! Mr. Vogel's hurt!"

One man came running while his friend called on his cell phone. The man checked to see if Mr. Vogel was breathing and if he had a pulse. Zack showed him the bruise that was now rising into a lump on the side of Mr. Vogel's head. A small crowd began to form. Zack saw a golf ball in the grass, not too far from Mr. Vogel. It wasn't Zack's!

"Maybe he was hit with this ball," Zack offered. "It could have come from the driving range. You know, if someone hit it *really* far."

One of the men picked it up. "Where did you find this?"

Zack showed him the spot on the ground where the grass was still flat from the ball.

"If this ball came from the direction of the driving range it wouldn't have hit him here, and landed there," said the man.

"It looks like it came from that direction," said a woman in the gathering crowd. She pointed back to the grove of trees. Zack was so confused. He hadn't seen anyone. The ball seemed to have come out of the clear blue sky.

Soon the ambulance showed up. The paramedics put Mr. Vogel on a stretcher. Zack felt sick. Mr. Vogel hadn't opened his eyes since he had watched Zack sink his last putt.

Zack picked up his clubs and the balls and ran home. When he got there, he called his mom and told her what had happened. She left work and was on her way home. It was then that Zack focused on the Magic Dozen.

"Did any of you see anything?" he asked them.

"No Zack, I'm sorry. I've already asked everyone. No one saw a thing." Linx informed him.

"What am I gonna do?" Zack started crying. He was scared. He loved Mr. Vogel and couldn't stand to think about him in the hospital. Worse was not knowing if Mr. Vogel was going to be okay.

Zack paced through the apartment. He couldn't sit still. More than anything he wanted his mom to come home and take him to the hospital. He tried to do some homework. He didn't feel like eating, and if he went for a jog he might miss his mom.

"Zack, everything happens for a reason. It *will* work out. Mr. Vogel is strong. Just try to breathe." Linx wanted to help, but nothing could calm Zack.

Finally, Zack's mom came bursting through the door. She knew what Mr. Vogel meant to Zack, and she had always been grateful that Mr. Vogel was there for him.

"Get in the car. It's still running," she said. It wasn't until they were both buckled in that she reached over and hugged Zack. "Honey, I'm sure everything is going to be just fine."

Inside the hospital Zack and his mother were told that they couldn't see Mr. Vogel. No visitors were allowed. Zack let a few more tears run down his cheeks. Zack and his mom sat in the waiting room hoping to see the doctor.

After an hour they were finally told about Mr. Vogel's condition. He was in a coma. Zack didn't know what that meant until the doctor explained. They didn't know when Mr. Vogel would wake up, or how much damage his accident had caused. Everyone would have to wait.

At home Zack crawled into bed, eyes red and swollen from all of his tears. The balls were all sitting quietly on his nightstand, trying desperately to comfort him.

"What's gonna happen? Before today everything was perfect…He's my best friend…" Zack wailed.

"It is all going to work out. Don't forget that we're all still here. We'll fill in for Mr. Vogel until he comes back. He has given you so much knowledge and great practice tips. He's shared almost everything he knows about the game. Now you just have to remember. With *our* help, you'll get through this. And, with *your* help, Mr. Vogel will pull through."

"What? I can't help him?"

"You can keep your chin up. Keep working as hard as you have been. And you heard the doctor, talk to him. Not now, but in a few days, when they let you in, go sit with him and tell him how hard you're practicing," advised Linx.

8

A Gracious Offer

The next month was difficult.

Zack had been allowed to see Mr. Vogel two days after the accident. There were tubes everywhere, and Mr. Vogel didn't look good. Zack pretended Mr. Vogel was sleeping, and that he would wake up soon.

Every day after he practiced at the driving range, Zack went in to sit by Mr. Vogel. He explained his day to him. Zack never left until he couldn't think of another detail. Each night before he left, Zack asked Mr. Vogel the same questions. "Why did you bet your driving range on me? Why did you think I could do it?"

The balls came with him faithfully. They would walk all over Mr. Vogel, telling him to open his eyes and checking out all of the equipment in his room. Even Triple Bogey had started behaving in the hospital.

One night while Zack was studying with the balls, he made a statement he would later regret. "I am *so* glad summer is almost here! I can't wait to not have to see Johnny…or study."

"Oh no, Zack, we need to have a talk," said Linx. "You are still far behind your class in reading and spelling. The other subjects seem to be coming along for you, but this is no time to relax. This is time to step up. I heard your teacher talking about summer school in class the other day."

"What! No way! It's *summer*! No more school. Can't you see how much has changed? I had 10 kids say 'hi' to me today! 10! That is about five more than ever before and eight more than usual! Everything's better. I don't need summer school," Zack cried.

"Yes, you do. Just think of how proud Mr. Vogel will be when he wakes up! It's worth it Zack. This isn't just been about making friends, or the tournament. Those things will mean nothing if you let your schoolwork slide. An education is so important. Look at how much confidence you've gotten since we started reading together. We all heard you read out loud in class the other day. There was only one word that tripped you up. You need to keep going." By this time all the other balls had heard their conversation and were gathering around.

"Ya know Laddie, ya can consider summer school like a little do over. The time ya spent not tryin is goin to be given back to ya. Like a do over. It's genius!" Mulligan said with a huge smile.

"We'll help you. It's the only way Zack," said Linx.

Zack left his room and walked out to the living room. He sat down and turned on the television. For what seemed like an eternity, Linx had been forbidding him to turn on the television except on the weekends after everything else was finished.

He sat down and turned on what used to be his favorite show. After watching for a few minutes he thought about the fact that Linx never let him have a soda during the week. On Linx's new program, Zack could have one soda on Sunday. He got up, went to the refrigerator and grabbed a can. He sat back down and took a long sip. When his show was over he turned off the television, finished his soda, and went back to his room.

"Feel better, do ya?" Mulligan asked.

"Yeah, I do. Do you?" Zack shot back.

"We'll all feel better once ya decide to go to summer school."

"I know, I know, I know. I guess you're right, but that doesn't mean I have to be happy about it." He turned his back and climbed in bed. Small cheers came from behind him. Clearly they were excited. Zack hoped he would be too, maybe tomorrow.

Zack had to drag himself to school the next day, knowing that the end of the year was no longer two weeks away. He had been counting down the days till summer. Now with summer school, there was little to look forward to. The Magic Dozen would definitely keep him working hard and playing less.

Zack got to class a little early so he could ask Mrs. Korey about summer school. The balls were once again in his bag, and he knew he would never hear the end of it if he didn't find out right away.

"Mrs. Korey, I have a question," Zack said as soon as he entered his classroom.

"Yes, what is it Zack?"

"I was kinda thinkin' about summer school." Mrs. Korey was shocked.

"Your grades have been coming up Zack. I have been impressed by your work over the last two months. Do your parents want you in summer school?"

"No, I just thought that since I've been trying harder and my grades are getting better I should keep it up, ya know?"

Zack had a really tough time trying to think of a way to explain his desire for summer school. He really couldn't say that the golf balls in his backpack were making him! Although, seeing his teacher's reaction to that answer might be worth it.

"Wow, Zack, it's wonderful to see you're making such an effort in your school work. Mr. Barnes is going to be teaching the summer program this year. It will start two weeks after school lets out, and it will be a month long. He will be covering each subject and assigning homework. It will be tough, but if you're willing to work hard, you could really benefit from his teaching." Mrs. Korey was smiling.

"Thanks. How do I sign up?"

"I'll take care of it. I will let Mr. Barnes know today, and your name will be on his list. I'm proud of you."

"Thanks," Zack said as he hung his head and went back outside to the playground until the first bell rang. He sat down at his favorite place. It was underneath a large tree right next to the track he had been running on for the last two months.

He looked around to make sure he was alone. Zack unzipped his bag and reached in and grabbed out the box of balls. Lost Ball was already scrambling to open his end of the box and climb out. "I know where we are guys! We must be at the driving range," Lost Ball exclaimed. Zack laughed.

"Lost, we have been here so many times. Recognize the track?"

"Yes, I do. Um, I was just testing you," said Lost.

"Right. Because you *always* know where you are, don't you?" Zack joked.

"Yes, thank you Zack, I *do* always know where I am. At least someone knows how wonderful my sense of direction is." The other balls laughed. Mulligan patted Lost on the back.

"Did you guys hear what Mrs. Korey said? It's going to be hard, there is *homework* and it lasts for an entire month!"

"You know Zack, the strong get stronger when they exercise their muscles." Linx said.

"What's that supposed to mean?"

"Just think of your brain as a muscle. The harder you exercise it, the stronger it will get. And that's true strength Zack. You just have to discipline yourself as hard as you have with your practicing, your running, and your eating habits," instructed Linx.

"Is that all?"

"I know it sounds like a lot. But you've come really far. This is no time to get discouraged. If you were going to give up, you should have done it at the beginning. You would've saved all of us a whole lot of trouble. Don't you think?" asked Linx.

"I'm not going to give up. I just don't want to go to summer school."

The bell rang and Zack headed inside with the other kids.

That night, on his way to visit Mr. Vogel, Zack noticed how many times he had pulled his pants up during the day. He finally had to tighten his belt. He also noticed how short his pants were getting. This was not a problem he was used to having. His mom always bought him new pants when they got too short and too tight, not because he couldn't keep them up. This was a new challenge, one he welcomed.

Zack walked into Mr. Vogel's room carrying the balls in his backpack. Zack found his chair in exactly the same spot he had left it the day before. If Mr. Vogel had visitors during the day, sometimes his chair would have been moved out of the room or to another spot in the room. No one must have come by today. Zack started and ended his conversation the same each day. It was only the details that changed.

"Mr. Vogel, its Zack. How are you today?" Zack didn't expect an answer. "Did I have a chance to tell you about summer school yet?"

The only sound in the room was the constant, steady beep of the heart monitor that was attached to Mr. Vogel's chest. He closed his eyes tightly and wished Mr. Vogel would answer him. He wanted to know what Mr. Vogel thought and what Mr. Vogel wanted him to do next. He wanted to hear Mr. Vogel call him "son" and pat him on the shoulder. Mr. Vogel just didn't look the same without his friendly smile stretched across his face, and in that silent moment, Zack missed the sound of Mr. Vogel's laugh. Zack squeezed Mr. Vogel's hand and waited for him to return the favor.

"Why did you bet your driving range on me? Why did you think I could do it? How could you be so sure this would all work out?"

Zack hadn't noticed the balls roaming around the room. They had slipped out through the half closed zipper.

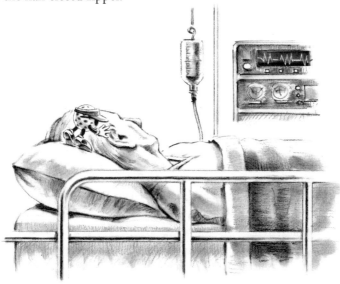

After asking his usual questions, Zack noticed Linx sitting on Mr. Vogel's pillow. He was talking quietly, gesturing with his hands. "What are you doing Linx?"

"I'm just talking to Mr. Vogel. I was letting him know how much you need him. I thought it might help if he could hear it from someone else too," said Linx.

"I thought you said no one else can see or hear you guys except me?"

"That's true. Maybe it's not my words that will help; maybe it's something we can't explain. He may never see or hear me, but maybe he can *feel* me…like I'm sure he *feels* you," Linx said.

Zack was quiet for awhile. "Maybe."

The next week at school was full of excitement. Zack could feel the buzz in the air as the kids grew eager for summer vacation. Zack was headed to class a few minutes early after lunch when he heard his name called on the loud speaker. He was being asked to report to the gym. What was going on? He hadn't had any problems with Johnny Beam for the last few weeks. He had never been called on the loud speaker for anything before. He felt nervous and uncertain as he made his way through the halls. Mr. Barnes was standing in the gym dribbling a basketball. He was the only one around. Zack opened the door and slipped inside. *What would Mr. Barnes need me for?*

"Did you call me Mr. Barnes?" Zack asked.

"Yes, good to see you. Why don't you come over here and have a seat on the bleachers with me. I want to talk to you." Zack and Mr. Barnes walked over and sat down. Zack noticed his palms were sweating.

"A few things have been brought to my attention. First of all, Mrs. Korey tells me you are enrolled in my summer school program. Is that correct?"

"Yes, sir," Zack answered.

"I've also been told that you are not required to, but you chose to."

Zack didn't say anything. He just shook his head slowly up and down.

"If that's not enough, I've noticed a physical change in you. You are working harder on all of your skills in my class. I see that you have been losing some weight. Last Saturday, I saw you running on the track. Needless to say, I'm impressed," said Mr. Barnes.

Zack could feel his face getting warmer. He knew that by now his cheeks were most likely a rosy shade of red. He felt embarrassed that anyone had seen him.

"I heard about your friend, Mr. Vogel. By now the word has begun to spread about you being involved in the city tournament. It must be really hard to practice now that Mr. Vogel is in the hospital. I'm sorry."

Zack felt Linx climbing onto his leg. Soon Linx was perched on Zack's shoulder, staring at Mr. Barnes. Then he leaned close to Zack's ear and whispered,

"My my, it seems you've become somewhat…what's the word…*popular?*" said Linx. Zack didn't answer, but he was smiling inside.

"Anyway, a really good friend of mine owns Emerald Pond, just 10 blocks south of here. It's the golf course that's holding the tournament." said Mr. Barnes.

"Yeah, I know. It's cool. I walked past it once, but I've never played there," Zack explained.

"Well, I told my friend, Mr. Austin, about you. He has extended a very gracious offer. He wants you to know that from now until the tournament, you are welcome to practice there free of charge. You can just walk onto the course as long as it's not too busy. He wanted to help. If you'd like I can take you over there after school, and I'll introduce you. It's about time you start playing on a real course, don't you think?" asked Mr. Barnes.

Zack was stunned. What should he say? Was he ready to play on a real course?

"Thhhank you, Mr. Barnes! Are you sure?"

Mr. Barnes laughed. "Of course. I'm honored that I could help. I'll meet you in the parking lot after school." Mr. Barnes got up and started walking towards his office.

Just as Zack stood up the bell rang. He hurried to class with only one thing on his mind. Butterflies took over his stomach. *What would Mr. Vogel say*? He couldn't wait to tell him.

Zack opened his backpack to find Linx. Linx had been waiting and jumped out as soon as the zipper opened. "Zack, this is great! Are you excited?"

"Yeah, I'm excited! Can you believe this?" asked Zack.

"Yes, I can. When you work hard and *run* in the right direction, good things just keep happening. When you have a positive attitude and believe for the best, the best will come your way. Of course, there are still tough times to go through, like what's happening to Mr. Vogel. But if you keep on believing, even the bad things can turn into good things," encouraged Linx.

"Thanks. I just wish I could tell Mr. Vogel."

"You can tell Mr. Vogel, same as you tell him what's happening every day," suggested Linx.

Emerald Pond was as wonderful as the golf courses Zack had seen on television. The greens were perfectly manicured, and the rolling hills were unbelievable. The course had perfectly raked sand traps and ponds where ducks floated lazily. It was awesome.

Mr. Barnes introduced Zack to Mr. Austin. Mr. Austin immediately offered his hand and said "Nice to meet you Zack, I have heard a lot about you. I was sorry to hear about Mr. Vogel. We have been friends for years."

Even though Mr. Austin ran one of the most prestigious private golf clubs in the state, he was always looking for ways to help any junior player that was trying to improve.

"Mr. Barnes tells me that you are our latest up and comer. I like players that take the bull by the horns," said Mr. Austin.

Zack still couldn't believe he would be playing at Emerald Pond.

"Let me take you on a tour," Mr. Austin said as he turned and handed Zack's clubs to the bag drop manager.

Zack and Mr. Austin entered the main lobby of the club. Zack was amazed. He had never seen such a beautiful lobby. Golf paintings lined the interior walls leading to the dining room where all the tables had neatly been set for the night's dinner. Zack remembered Mr. Vogel talking about country clubs like this one, but he never thought he would be seeing one in person, let alone practicing here for free.

"Let's go downstairs to the locker room and get you checked in," Mr. Austin directed.

They walked into a room neatly lined with lockers, each one containing a name. Zack noticed one locker that was by itself on the aisle.

The plaque on the door read, JACK BEAM.

Zack shuddered as he walked past. Plaques and trophies were on display around the locker. The wall at the end had been dedicated to member tournament champions. He quickly noticed that both Johnny and Jack Beam's names were displayed numerous times. Johnny had been hailed a champion. Zack stared at one of the trophies as he imagined his name on the plaque instead of Johnny Beam's.

"I am going to put you in our junior section; here is your locker combination. Get settled in, and go warm up. The driving range is out that door and to your left. Once you are ready, come and see me. I have something for you." Mr. Austin smiled and went out the door. Zack changed clothes and went to the range.

Tucked safely in his pocket were Long Ball and Linx. Long Ball had begged for the opportunity to go flying on the fancy course. The others rode quietly in his golf bag for the moment, though Zack knew that was not where they'd stay.

This range was completely different than Mr. Vogel's. Instead of worn out rubber mats and concrete slabs, the practice area at Emerald Pond was neatly manicured with a carpet of green grass. There were no wire buckets for holding practice balls just neatly stacked pyramids. Zack picked up a ball and noticed that each one was new and displayed the Emerald Pond logo. He slipped a ball into his pocket anxious to show Mr. Vogel.

"I have been here before; I know I have," shouted Lost Ball. Zack just smiled.

"There's no time like the present to start playing in the big leagues!" Linx encouraged.

"I'm nervous," said Zack.

"Sure you are. But this is why you've been training."

Zack stood on the green. Deeply he breathed in the warm breeze. He stared straight ahead at the rolling landscape. He couldn't believe how small he felt on such a large course. He stepped up to send the new Emerald Pond golf ball to the first hole. The ball flew into the air, leaning much more to the left than Zack would have liked. He took another deep breath and pulled Linx out of his pocket.

"Okay, I don't want you helping me! I just want to try this shot again. You only get to go for a ride, but *no* helping!" Zack said.

"You've got it Champ. You really don't need the help, not to worry, I'm gonna let you decide where I go. Good luck," said Linx with a smile.

Linx kept his promise and the shot was much better. However, Zack was hoping Linx would have landed a little closer to the hole than he did. *I think having this big course is throwing off my game! Good thing I get to practice here...*

Zack continued to practice on the first two holes before going to find Mr. Austin. "I have something for you that might help you understand the course," Mr. Austin said. He handed him a small spiral notebook with all 18 holes outlined: yardage distances, sand trap locations, water hazards, and green information. It was marked with notes and tips on how to play each hole. Zack had never seen printed information for a golf course before. It was so detailed and seemed to explain everything.

"One should always prepare before one plays, wouldn't you agree?" said Mr. Austin as he winked and walked away.

Zack read through the information and started back at the first hole. By the time he reached the third hole, he was beginning to relax. He was only a few over par and was excited to see where he'd be when he finished the course.

"Is that Jelly Belly over there?" he heard someone yell. He turned to see Johnny and his friends. Zack tried to continue playing through the insults. Within seconds Johnny and his friends walked up next to him.

Before they got there Triple Bogey yelled, "Let us at them, we'll handle this." Zack had let all of the balls know that he wanted to fight this battle on his own. He felt confident knowing that they were there in case he got himself in trouble.

Johnny shoved Zack's golf bag, sending his clubs crashing to the ground. Thankfully all of the balls had gotten out before and were spread all around Zack, Linx was on his shoulder.

"What do you think you're doing here Fatty?" Johnny asked.

"Mr. Austin told me I could start practicing here. Until the tournament, I'm allowed to come whenever I want."

Johnny was angry. He threw down his club and started shouting, "What do you mean, you're 'allowed to come whenever you want'?! Don't tell me I have to share my course with YOU!"

Zack just stood there. He watched Johnny throw a fit.

"You're too *fat* to play here. Didn't you read the sign on the front door? No *fat losers* allowed!" Zack felt his confidence melting.

"Well, um, Johnny, I don't know if you can really call him 'fat' anymore," one of Johnny's friends said. "Besides, what'd he ever do to you anyway?"

Zack could not believe what he was hearing. Johnny spun around to face his friend. *Did someone just stick up for me?*

"What! Of course I can. He's still fat! He'll always be fat."

"Look at him; he's not really that fat anymore. But he's gettin' bigger. He's almost as tall as you are. Maybe you're gonna have to think of something different to call him," said Johnny's friend.

"I'll call him whatever I want!" Johnny shouted. He picked up his club and marched off. His friends followed behind him, but they kept a safe distance. Zack took a deep breath.

"Did you hear that Laddie? They don't think you're fat! It looks like your image is goin' to be gettin' a second chance. Isn't this excitin'?" Mulligan asked.

"Yeah," Zack said slowly.

9

Remember THIS!

Zack lay in bed on the morning of the last day of school thinking about the summer ahead. He would do summer school for a month and still have some time to practice from morning until dark before the tournament. Running wasn't as tough as before. His game was improving. His mom had celebrated his recent weight loss and his good grades by buying him a few pairs of shorts and a pair of pants that were his new size.

Mr. Vogel still wasn't getting better, but he wasn't getting any worse either. The balls had kept Zack working harder than ever before. They had become such good friends that he could hardly remember life without them.

"Linx, I've been thinking. Remember when you said, 'Every day you miss practicing, it will take you one day longer to get good?'"

"Yes, I remember."

"Did you know Ben Hogan or not? I have to know!"

"Zack, everyone is great at something. You have become great at jogging, eating healthier foods, golfing, and doing your school work."

"I'm not great; I've just gotten a little better," Zack confessed.

"Well, maybe someone who wasn't as good as you are right now would think that you are great. It just depends on who you are and where you're at. Do you understand?"

"I guess. But that doesn't tell me if you knew Ben Hogan."

"Look at the time boy; you're going to find yourself late to your last day of school. Quick, quick, let's get you going," said Linx.

With a heavy sigh, Zack got out of bed. He had gotten used to Linx's various distractions whenever he would ask about Ben Hogan. *Maybe I'll never know for sure.*

At school Zack walked down the hall for the last time that year. Summer school would be held in the building out back. He had started the year as a shy, quiet, chubby kid who had always been picked on. He was ending the year as the not-so-quiet, still a little shy, less chubby, taller, borderline smart kid who was only occasionally getting picked on. It was an improvement.

His thoughts were interrupted by a familiar voice. "Hey Fatty! Don't forget that I'm the *best*! You'll never be able to beat me. My dad will be getting the driving range. Those new condos will look awesome on Mr. Vogel's property," Johnny yelled.

"Well, we'll see Johnny. By the end of the summer you might wish you could play at Mr. Vogel's new course." Zack had never had a comeback for anything Johnny had said. Zack heard a few kids start to laugh. Johnny's face turned red with anger.

"Enjoy your summer Tubby! I can't wait to crush you at the tournament!"

In two weeks Zack had only seen Johnny on the course one time. Mr. Austin had told Zack that Johnny hadn't been coming around very much. Johnny had gone on a family vacation. Since he had been back, no one at Emerald Pond had seen him. Zack was glad.

Summer school started. It wasn't as bad as Zack had thought. He had kept up his reading to the Magic Dozen in the evenings. In the past two weeks Mulligan had been helping him even more with his math skills.

Mr. Barnes was a good teacher. Besides teaching, Mr. Barnes had offered to drop Zack off at the golf course every day after school. He had to pass Emerald Pond on his way home, so Zack had accepted the offer.

Zack also kept up his routine of seeing Mr. Vogel every day. Half way through his month of summer school, he opened Mr. Vogel's door to find the room full of nurses and doctors. They were all standing over Mr. Vogel. Zack's stomach knotted instantly. He sat on his chair that had been shoved into the corner and drew his legs up to his chest. He wrapped his arms around his knees and waited. It seemed like forever before anyone noticed he was there.

"Zack, we are going to need you to step outside for just a few minutes," one of the nurses said.

"What's wrong? Is he going to be okay?" Zack questioned.

"The boy's fine. Let him stay. He's here every day," one of the doctors said. Almost a half hour went by before anyone talked to Zack again.

"Come over here Zack, I want you to see this." Zack hadn't realized anybody at the hospital knew his name. A nurse took Zack over to Mr. Vogel. He could see that Mr. Vogel's eyes were half open. The nurse said, "Do you see his eyes? He opened them half way this evening. That happened about the same time he squeezed his doctor's hand."

"He squeezed the doctor's hand?"Zack shouted.

"Yes, shhh, he did. It wasn't very hard, but he did respond." Zack was so overwhelmed that tears filled his eyes. Again, Linx was sitting on his pillow. Zack saw Mulligan and Birdie watching from their spot on top of one of the machines next to Mr. Vogel. Zack broke down and cried. All he wanted was for Mr. Vogel to be able to make it to the tournament.

Summer school was over. Zack had been so busy that the time flew by. He had his highest test score ever on the final exam. He had "B"s in every subject. This was a huge difference from his usual "D"s and occasional "F"s.

Each day Zack practiced at Emerald Pond. Mr. Austin told Zack that some of the members had noticed how much he had improved. Even Johnny had asked about him. Zack smiled. Apparently Johnny had been practicing every day since he had received the news.

Two days before the tournament, Mr. Vogel still had not woken up. He had improved but he was still in bed, unable to move. Zack had been sitting next to Mr. Vogel pleading with him to get up every day of the last week. He knew his mom would be at the tournament, and Mr. Barnes said he wouldn't miss it for the world. Zack wanted Mr. Vogel to be there most of all.

Tournament day finally arrived, and Zack reached the golf course early to begin his warm up routine. He noticed the change in the atmosphere at Emerald Pond. An excitement had filled the air. Junior players, parents, and coaches were buzzing around, awakening Emerald Pond.

Zack had grown accustomed to having the Magic Dozen with him constantly. He wondered if he should have left some of them behind and only brought a few. But each one had helped him at one time or another, and leaving any one of them behind was not an option.

Linx interrupted his thoughts as he jumped from Zack's backpack onto his shoulder. "You've made it! You deserve to be here. How does it feel?"

"I don't know if I should be here. I don't know if I can win."Zack answered.

"Go back to the beginning. Do you remember when Mr. Vogel asked you about what you wanted? This is your time to shine. If you knew without a doubt that you were going to win, what kind of fun would that be? Now pick up your clubs and let's show everyone what you're made of. We're wasting perfectly good warm up time."

Zack walked out on the range to find several junior players warming up. He was familiar with some of them, but there were others he didn't know. Johnny and his friends were at the end of the range hitting balls when they turned and spotted Zack.

"Hey Loser, why did you even show up today?" shouted Johnny. Zack's world froze instantly.

"Remember this?" Johnny took a half swing and sent a ball bouncing down the range toward Zack. The ball stopped just short of hitting him. Zack walked to the ball, took a 4 iron out of his bag, and glared back at Johnny. Zack whispered for Long Ball. Then, he shouted back at Johnny.

"I think you should remember *this* while you're playing today!" Zack turned, looked straight down the range, and then focused on the ball sitting on the tee. Zack took a full swing, and the ball rocketed off his club easily passing the 200 yard maker. All the players stood in amazement, including Johnny.

"All the junior players for the City Tournament please report in," came the request over the loudspeaker. Zack picked up his bag and headed toward the score table where Mr. Austin was watching the players check in.

"Good morning players, and welcome to Emerald Pond for the Annual City Junior Tournament," announced Mr. Austin. "Today we are playing a single elimination match play event with the winner moving to the next round. If there is a tie after the 18 holes, you will play a sudden death hole, or holes, until a winner is determined. You will be playing from the white tees today. I expect each one of you to play well and play fair. Are there any questions?" No hands were raised.

Zack looked up at the scoreboard and noticed that he was paired with Tyler Edmonds, and his tee-off time was in 15 minutes.

"Next on the number one tee, Zack and Tyler," rang through the air.

"I'm ready," said Zack to Linx.

On the tee box, Tyler won the toss and elected to hit first. His shot was good. It landed on the left side of the fairway. Zack placed his ball on the tee and a flood of memories filled his mind. He remembered Mr. Vogel and all he had taught him. He thought of his new friends, especially Linx. He thought of all the work he had done to get to this point. He had been busy. He had learned how to discipline himself.

Zack moved his club back in a perfect swing and followed through. Zack's ball flew past Tyler's by 40 yards and landed dead center of the fairway. The players waiting to tee off next were stunned. Zack could hear them whispering.

"Even Johnny can't hit that far. Who's this Zack kid?"

Johnny overheard their comments and shouted, "He's the fatty trying to golf! He's nobody, and he can't play! He's a loser." For the first time, Johnny's shouting fell on deaf ears. One of the players yelled back, "I wish I could hit a ball like that! What's the matter Johnny, afraid someone's better than you?" Johnny stormed off, but no one followed.

During the round Zack and Tyler discussed golf, practicing, and recalled the day's great shots. Tyler was no competition for Zack. Zack was thrilled as he walked down the fairway. Not only was he playing a great game, but he was doing something he had never done before; making a friend. One that other people could see too. By the end of the day, Zack had beaten Tyler by 10 strokes.

"I hope I can play as good as you some day. You're an awesome player." said Tyler.

"Thanks."

"Did you hear that Zack? You are da man, just like I am *Da Man*!!!" The Magic Dozen chanted, "Zack is da man! Zack is da man!" Zack laughed, wishing for a moment that everyone around him could hear the miniature choir.

Mr. Barnes and Zack's mother were standing off to the side of the eighteenth green. Mr. Barnes was clapping, and Zack's mother was holding back tears of joy as she watched her son win. It was the first time anything like this had ever happened for Zack. When she could no longer hold back, she took off running towards Zack. Her congratulations hug threatened to smother him.

Mr. Barnes followed her over and shook Zack's hand. "Great job, Zack! I knew you could do it."

"Zack, I am so proud of you!" his mother exclaimed.

Zack was standing in a fog of compliments. Mr. Barnes and his mother gushed about his success, and he noticed he could still hear the balls. Together, these were his greatest fans, but one was missing.

"Zack! Zack," said Linx, tugging on his pant leg. "Go turn in your score card, and make sure you sign it. We have more practicing to do."

"What? More practicing? I just finished and I won. Linx, I won!" said Zack.

"This is only the *first* round and you have two more rounds before you face Johnny. I have a feeling that the next ones will be much, much harder. I don't have a good feeling about playing Kevin Hester; you know he is one of Johnny's friends," said Linx.

"Mom, I think I'm gonna stay and practice a little. Can you pick me up later?"

"Are you sure you want to stay and practice?"

"Yeah."

Just then Mr. Austin walked over. "One round at a time, that's the way to do it…take a round at a time." He said with a wink. "You play again tomorrow at 9 o'clock. Kevin is a little better player than Tyler. Remember, all the *great* players continually practice, *especially* after they just finished winning a round."

During practice Zack could feel all his nerves relaxing for a moment. He hadn't realized how scared he had really been. One wrong move could end this whole bet in a flash.

"Hey Zack, maybe I could jump up on the tee for a shot, it's been awhile…" said Linx.

"Sure," Zack answered excitedly.

Linx bounced onto the tee and tucked in his little arms and legs. Just as Zack got into his stance Long Ball called out, "Go flyin' man, enjoy! Bet you can't go as far as I can…although if you just imagine that pretty little Teena is on the other side of that cup, you might just make it." All the balls roared. Linx rolled his eyes.

"That's the second time I've heard about Teena," said Zack.

"Yeah, well, ignore them, they think they're really funny. Come on Zack, send me to the moon!"

Zack scooted his chair next to Mr. Vogel. "Mr. Vogel, I won, I won my first round! Now only three more to go, and you'll have your golf course! Mr. Vogel please wake up!" Mr. Vogel continued to lie silently. Zack pulled out his Emerald Pond ball and slipped it into his hand. Mr. Vogel's fingers slowly closed around the ball. Zack jumped.

From the pillow Linx yelled, "Zack, his hand moved! He's holding the ball! Zack!" Linx had snapped his fingers to get Zack's attention. "You're *not* seeing things Zack, Mr. Vogel is holding the ball!"

"Mom, Mom!" shouted Zack. "Did you see that? Mr. Vogel's hand moved. Look! He's holding the Emerald Pond golf ball! Get the nurse!" Zack was immediately thankful that his mother had insisted on coming with him.

The nurse walked in to find Mr. Vogel grasping the ball. "This is a wonderful sign, Zack. Keep talking to him. All we can do is see what happens."

Zack was in tears. He could feel his mother's arm around his shoulders. With her encouragement he began talking to Mr. Vogel. He told him everything. Especially how Tyler had said he wished he could play as good as Zack. As he talked, Zack searched Mr. Vogel's face for any sign that Mr. Vogel could hear him. He tried squeezing Mr. Vogel's hand again. There was no more movement.

Zack sat down in his chair and watched as Linx spoke to Mr. Vogel. Zack was sure Mr. Vogel couldn't hear Linx. Even Triple Bogey looked excited about the progress. They stood at the end of the bed, staring at Mr. Vogel's frozen hand. Zack saw Lost Ball rifling through the box of Kleenex. Zack watched tearfully as Lost delivered tissues to him and Linx. Then Lost put one on top of Zack's mother's purse. Zack picked it up and handed it to his mom.

"Thank you, baby," she said softly. "This has really been a great day. Tomorrow could be even better. Let's go home."

Zack lay in bed replaying the entire day. Images from the day that Mr. Vogel had made the bet flooded his mind. Zack had known at that very moment that his life had changed forever. He leaned over, looking at the 12 balls neatly tucked away in their box and whispered, "Thank you."

Back at Emerald Pond, the tournament was getting exciting. Zack and Kevin were tied after the first four holes and the long par five was next. Zack knew he needed to stay far left on his tee shot or the ball would roll down the hill into the woods. Kevin's ball started straight off the tee box and then faded right. The ball bounced once and then plunged deeply into the woods. The ball was definitely lost.

Linx had told Zack to pay attention to the balls that Kevin used. They were Wilson balls with three red dots under the logo. Zack waited, trying to give Kevin enough time to find his ball.

When Kevin shouted, "Found it," from the edge of the woods all the balls stared at each other. Each one started shouting,

"There's no way!"

"It couldn't be!"

"He's cheating, Zack!"

Linx said, "Hey, has anyone seen Lost Ball?" Everyone looked around.

"Triple Bogey is missing too, Laddie," said Mulligan.

Kevin hit his next shot down the fairway.

Zack hit his next shot and it landed 125 yards from the green. Walking past Kevin, Zack noticed that the ball he was using was different. It was a Dunlop. The Magic Dozen noticed too.

"He is indeed cheating! Keep your focus Zack." said Linx. Just then the balls spotted Lost coming out of the woods, "I found Kevin's ball. I can always find lost balls. My directional sense is perfect!" For once Lost Ball had come through for the team. He had been *lost* in the right place at the right time.

"Let us at him, we'll make him pay!" shouted Triple Bogey as they emerged from behind Lost Ball.

"No! Guys, I have to figure out what to do," said Zack. He wasn't sure what he should say. It was obvious what Kevin had done. *Whose gonna believe me?* He couldn't prove it. "Linx, what should I do?"

"Normally, Zack, you would tell the tournament director or roving marshal."

Linx thought for a moment and then said, "Zack, concentrate on *your* play, and leave the rest to us. He started this, and we will finish it. Cheating is not allowed. It's time that Kein learns this very valuable lesson.

10

"What's Your Game Plan?"

Both Zack and Kevin were 100 yards from the pin on their third shot. A small pond located directly in front of the green made the first shot very important. Zack hit first and his ball flew over the pond, landing in the center of the green.

Linx looked at Wet and nodded. Wet knew his time had come. Kevin pulled back his club and hit. Before his club connected with the ball, Wet had strategically placed himself over Kevin's ball. Zack watched as the ball headed for the green and suddenly dropped short into the water. He laughed quietly to himself as he saw Wet's arms and legs spread out while he yelled, "Cool, refreshing, beautiful water… *here I come!*" To everyone else it just looked like Kevin's ball, but from where Zack stood, it looked like justice.

"Tough break," said Zack as he walked toward the green. Kevin hit another ball and again it splashed in the water. This time, no help from the Magic Dozen.

Kevin ended up taking a nine on that hole.

The tournament continued and every time Kevin cheated, he paid dearly. His game seemed to worsen each time he cheated. By the end of the day, Zack had beaten Kevin by 14 strokes.

After signing his score card, Zack turned it into Mr. Austin. For the second time in two days, congratulations were given. It was also the second time that Zack heard Mr. Austin giving him the same advice that Linx had echoed the day before. "Great job Zack, I knew you could do it! But, don't get too excited, you still have two more rounds to win. One round at a time, that's the way to do it. Take a round at a time. You play again tomorrow at 9:15 a.m. It's you and Jeff Cousley."

Zack headed for the club's snack bar to get a bite to eat before he continued practicing. "Linx, I really thought that once I made it to the tournament, I wouldn't have to be practicing so much. It seems like I am playing more golf in a day, now that the tournament has started, than I did before," said Zack.

Linx popped out of Zack's pocket and landed on his shoulder.

"Welcome to 'being great,' Zack. You heard Mr. Austin. There is only one way great players are made, and it's by a little something called practice, practice, practice!" Linx must have found his comment hilarious because he leaned back and let out a loud laugh. Zack smiled too. It was clear that Zack had learned about that "something" over the last five months.

To get to the snack bar he cut through the locker room. Soon after entering he thought he heard someone say his name. He stopped, carefully listening. It was Kevin and Johnny. He could tell they were arguing. As the discussion became more intense, their voices got louder. It was obvious that their disagreement was about the day's tournament.

"I *tried!*" said Kevin. "But every time I cheated, I got worse. My game was worse than it's ever been. I don't know why I ever listened to you! Do your own dirty work next time. Besides, what do you have against him? He seems nice and he's really good."

Johnny slammed his hand against the locker. "OKAY THEN! GO BE THE LOSER'S FRIEND!"

"MAYBE I WILL!" shouted Kevin. "MAYBE I WILL! And by the way, I'm going to tell David NOT to listen to you!" From where Zack stood he could hear Kevin kicking lockers and slamming doors as he left the locker room.

Zack and his mother eagerly walked into Mr. Vogel's room. Inside they saw the nurses surrounding him. They seemed different, more excited than the previous nights when Zack had come to visit.

"Zack, come look! Mr. Vogel is making progress."

Zack went over to the bed to find Mr. Vogel's hand tightly holding the Emerald Pond golf ball. Anyone trying to take it away from him was meeting surprising resistance.

"He is trying Zack! This is great!" said the nurse.

Zack looked over at his mom. She knew the drill. It was now time for her to step outside so Zack could talk privately with Mr. Vogel. She had done this since the beginning.

Zack leaned over to Mr. Vogel's ear and started talking.

"I am so nervous! I'm really excited about beating Kevin, but I'm not done. Please wake up. Wake up!" Mr. Vogel lay still. "Mr. Vogel, I'm gonna take the ball out of your hand. Can I have it?" Zack reached for the ball that was tightly held in Mr. Vogel's hand. Slowly, the hand opened.

"You *can* hear me! Do you want it back?" Zack carefully placed the ball back in the palm of Mr. Vogel's hand. Slowly, just as before, his fingers moved and grasped the ball.

The balls started bouncing up and down throughout the room shouting, "Mr. Vogel; he's da man. He's da man." Linx stayed in his place on Mr. Vogel's pillow. He smiled and continued whispering into Mr. Vogel's ear.

Zack woke up early the next morning feeling great. He got ready and headed to Emerald Pond, arriving before any other players. Only four players were left in the tournament, and as each day passed, the crowd got bigger. At one time, this would have bothered Zack.

"Zack, I need to speak with you," said Linx from his usual perch on his shoulder. "Today is going to be tough, and I want to make sure that you are ready. Jeff Cousley was last year's runner up, and he is a very good player. So far, you have done well, and I am very proud. You need to know he is much better than Tyler or Kevin. This will not be easy."

"Just watch me today," said Zack. "Jeff doesn't stand a chance."

"Zack, listen to me. Don't underestimate Jeff, and don't overestimate your abilities. Please, listen."

Zack looked at Linx, "Don't worry so much Linx. I've been thinking about it, and I'm ready. The last two days are proof! In fact, today I am feeling so good that all of you could probably even take a break and just watch me from the sidelines."

"Okay, Zack." Linx just shook his head as Zack went to the tee box.

"On the first tee we have Zack and Jeff," announced the loudspeaker.

Zack won the toss and teed off. His ball sailed straight down the fairway. The crowd clapped and Zack smiled. Now it was Jeff's turn. He pulled his club back and rhythmically hit the ball. Jeff's ball headed straight down the fairway and passed Zack's by 25 yards.

Zack was shocked. No one had out driven him in the tournament.

The next few holes consisted of back and forth play between the boys. Both were making good shots. Zack would hit a great shot and Jeff would counter, hitting one even better. Zack was playing an aggressive competitor that would not give in…or give up.

Zack had started to feel the pressure of the day. By the ninth hole he was behind by two strokes. "Linx? Linx, where are you?" he said quietly. Linx did not appear. Zack remembered how he had dismissed all the balls early that morning. *Of course they wouldn't take me seriously? Right?* His over-confidence had clouded his judgment. Suddenly he felt very alone.

Zack started thinking about losing, *"…What if I never even get to the finals? What if I lose and Mr. Vogel loses everything? What if I…"*

"Don't go there!" came the warning from behind Zack's bag.

"Linx, I'm so glad you're here! I'm sorry. Please help me. Jeff is really good and I'm behind!"

"The first thing you need to do is calm down. We have another nine holes where you can make up two shots. It can be done if you hold on and concentrate. Next, think only positive thoughts. Visualize each shot being hit perfectly. Last, always review your notes and take each shot one at a time. Remember, play each shot one at a time. Now let's get started."

Zack tried to regain his confidence. Linx was right, "I have nine holes to make up two shots. Just take it one shot at a time," he said out loud.

The competitive battle continued between Jeff and Zack. By the end of the sixteenth hole, Zack had tied Jeff. Only two holes remained to determine who would reach the finals and who would go home. The problem in Zack's mind was that there was more at stake for him. The difference was that one of them would just go home, and the other would go home knowing Mr. Vogel's life had been changed forever.

The last two holes had not been good for Zack. The last two days he had bogied both of them, and today he needed to play better. The seventeeth hole offered a par three on an island green, and the eighteenth was a long par five with a dogleg left, leading into a tucked away green near the clubhouse.

Zack looked intently at his notes, deciding how to play the hole. He could feel a gentle breeze coming over his left shoulder, and then he noticed the water. In the pond he saw a slight ripple skip across the surface. Then he turned to see the flag slowly waving.

"I can tell you feel the winds of change," Linx stated. Normally Zack would use a 7 iron from this distance, as he had the last two days. However, there hadn't been a breeze before. He changed his mind and decided on an 8 iron, hoping the breeze would help carry the ball to the hole.

Jeff was on the tee box and did not appear to notice the subtle change in the wind. He used his 7 iron and the ball flew past the pin, landing on the back edge of the green. The ball rolled down near the water.

Zack teed his ball and hit it with his 8 iron. He landed his shot ten feet from the pin where it rolled to four inches of the hole. Almost a hole in one!

Zack remembered what Linx and Mr. Vogel had told him, "always observe and feel your surroundings." At that moment, Zack remembered the drills Mr. Vogel had taught him during practice. The blindfold to help him *see* was especially helpful.

Zack birdied the hole and Jeff bogied it. Zack now led by two strokes. He teed off from the eighteenth hole, and his ball soared straight down the fairway. Jeff's shot soon followed, landing near Zack's ball.

Zack took out his book and studied for a moment. "Linx, I think I can cut the corner over the trees and be on the green." Linx just shook his head.

"Zack, chances should be taken when necessary. Is this one of those times?"

Zack thought a moment and then shook his head. He pulled out a 5 iron and hit the ball 100 yards short of the green.

Jeff made the decision to take the chance. He needed to hit above the trees to land his ball on the green. The ball had to travel almost 175 yards in the air. This was a difficult shot for an adult and much more difficult for a junior who wasn't as strong.

Jeff took out his 5 wood, aimed, and hit the ball perfectly. Zack and Linx watched as the ball cleared the trees and headed toward the green. On landing, Jeff's ball ended short. It landed in the bunker protecting the green.

Jeff's shoulders slumped, and he looked down at the ground. He knew at that moment his chances to win were gone.

Zack used his iron to hit his ball onto the green and then putted in for par. The crowd clapped, and Zack shook Jeff's hand.

"Good luck tomorrow. By the way, I wouldn't mind going out to practice with you some time," said Jeff.

"Yeah. Maybe next week?"

"Sure, see you around." Jeff replied.

Mr. Austin came over and shook hands with Zack. "You play for the City Championship at 1 o'clock tomorrow afternoon, and your opponent will be last year's champion, Johnny Beam. I know you two have already met! Good luck," said Mr. Austin.

Upon arriving at the hospital, something didn't seem right. There were no nurses in sight. Mr. Vogel was lying motionless in his bed. The normal beeping sound that Zack had become accustomed to was gone. The shades were closed, making it hard to see. Like thick fog, an eery feeling had settled over Mr. Vogel's room. Once Zack had taken it all in he shouted, "Oh, no! No!" He rushed over to the bed. He grabbed Mr. Vogel's hand with one of his, and placed his other hand on Mr. Vogel's chest. Zack shook Mr. Vogel. "Please wake up! Please!" Zack was crying. He feared the worst. A familiar voice interrupted his sobbing. It was quiet and very scratchy.

"Why are you in here instead of out practicing?"

"Mr. Vogel! Mr. Vogel, you're…you're…you're awake!"

"It takes more than a little bump on the head to keep me down," mumbled

Mr. Vogel. Zack drew in a huge breath as he felt an enormous weight lift off his shoulders. A new sense of relief washed over him as he stared at Mr. Vogel. Zack wiped his nose on his sleeve and sniffed.

"Well, don't just stare at me son, talk to me."

He told Mr. Vogel about everything he had missed since he had been in the hospital. Zack was eager to tell him about all of his training. He wanted to tell him about summer school, practicing at Emerald Pond, and about making friends. Most of all, he wanted to tell Mr. Vogel how well he was playing in the tournament.

"Stand up Zack and let me take a look at you." Mr. Vogel slowly turned his head and looked Zack over from top to bottom. "You're not Zack…not the one I remember anyway."

"What do you mean? It's me." Zack was confused. *Mr. Vogel does remember me, doesn't he? Is he still sick?*

"You have grown. Just look at all the weight you've lost and what are those?" Mr. Vogel asked as he pointed to Zack's forearms. "Are those muscles? No, you are not the Zack I know. But, I could grow to like this one too!"

"Mr. Vogel…" Zack felt embarrassed. Tears filled his eyes again as he stared down at his best friend.

"Now, let's talk about tomorrow. What's your game plan?" *Leave it Mr. Vogel to get right down to business.*

Zack showed him the course book. He explained how he had taken each hole one at a time, thinking about every shot.

"Anything else?" Mr. Vogel asked.

"Yes. I never underestimate any opponent."

"Nicely done! Sound's like Mr. Barnes has done a great job picking up where I left off." Zack swallowed hard. How could he explain about what really happened?

"Time to go. Mr. Vogel still needs to rest. He'll be back to the range in no time, but for now we need him quiet," said the head nurse.

"You come back tomorrow and tell him your good news. You know, the news about you winning the City Tournament. Good luck Zack." Zack started down the hallway.

"Zack, Zack," called Mr. Vogel. Zack turned and hustled back to the room.

"I'm here."

"I just wanted to say how proud I am of you. Whatever happens tomorrow, I know that you've won. I don't know how you did it son."

"Well, that's a long story. Maybe when you're feeling better."

"It seems like I remember someone else talking to me. Did you ever bring someone with you? Linx, I think it was?"

"You know Linx?" Zack questioned. Zack's eyes opened wide and his eyebrows rose.

"Well, I wouldn't say I know him. I just remember hearing someone talk, and he introduced himself as Linx. Come to think of it, I've heard you say that name before."

"Yeah, um, remember the box? Linx was the one I told you about…" Zack grimaced as he waited to hear Mr. Vogel's response.

"Hey, I told you I'd believe anything if you could learn to hit as well as you did when you first found the box. Clearly, you've learned a lot since I've been here. But, are you trying to tell me a *golf ball* was talking to me while I was sleeping?"

Zack shrugged. What else was he supposed to say?

"Surely stranger things have happened? But, do me a favor, and go win this tournament." Mr. Vogel started laughing. Then he said, "I know I heard a small voice. It was this Linx fellow. He felt close, almost like he was inside my head? I don't know what to think anymore. Just tell him 'thanks,' okay?"

"You just did." Zack turned to leave. A few steps down the hall Linx peeked out of Zack's shirt pocket and said, "I knew he could hear me!"

"How did he hear you, I thought no one else could?" asked Zack.

"Well, few people can see or hear us because they don't believe. You are our mission, and that's why it was easy for you. But, Mr. Vogel seemed to need us too, and you need him, so I just tried!"

11

The Locker Room

The final day of the tournament had come. The most important day of Zack's life was about to unfold. Behind the practice area a small group started forming, anxious to watch the two finalists practice.

Over the crowd's chatter a familiar voice called. "Well, I thought you might not show up, loser! I thought you'd be too afraid to take the beating I am going to give you today," shouted Johnny Beam. Zack ignored Johnny and continued to warm up.

"Hey, Zack, my dad said that I could help tear down that dump of a range after I win. In fact, my dad's already over there surveying the property. He'll be coming by to watch me win. That crazy Mr. Vogel had better stay in a coma so he won't have to see his star student lose!"

There was a time when Zack would've looked for the quickest exit and escaped. That was before. All the insults Johnny had hurled at him over the years had piled up. All the times that Johnny had made Zack feel bad came boiling out of his soul and showed on his face. Zack placed his club in his bag and started walking towards Johnny.

Johnny immediately saw a change in Zack. Zack's eyes had a steely look that focused directly on him. He continued to get closer, and Johnny realized that Zack's size and stature seemed much taller and tougher than he had remembered. The closer he got, the larger Zack looked. The overweight, timid kid had disappeared, and a tall, fit kid with a healthy dose of confidence had taken his place. Johnny took a few steps back as Zack continued to approach.

"NOT TODAY!" were the calm, loud words spoken by Zack. He had managed to speak with control even though everything in him wanted to scream. Zack stood staring at Johnny for more than a moment, and then he turned away and walked back to his clubs. Linx and the Magic Dozen were proud, and they knew then that Zack had officially overcome his fear of Johnny Beam and he wouldn't be bullied anymore.

Johnny didn't stop. He continued making comments. For the first time in Zack's or Johnny's lives, the name calling and rude comments didn't stick. Zack hardly noticed. He had other things to think about.

The crowd had moved away from Johnny and stood directly behind Zack offering encouraging words. "You can do it, Zack! Go out and win." And of course from the Magic Dozen came Zack's most cherished phrase, "Just *Be the ball*."

Zack turned to look at the balls. He laughed when he saw that Wet had taken the lid off of his water bottle and was now bobbing up and down in it. He looked up at Zack and waved. There was no sense in asking Wet to get out; he had earned his place. Next to him, as always, Beach had found a place in the sun where he had stretched out his chair as he "soaked up the rays." Triple Bogey was missing from the group. That wasn't a good sign. They got into trouble, but it could usually be fixed. After a quick scan of the area, Zack saw them climbing onto Johnny's golf bag. He whistled and nodded at Linx, who took off running in their direction.

"Players, please report to the clubhouse," came the request from the loud speaker.

The spectators started moving to the first tee to get a good spot to watch the play.

Zack placed his clubs in the rack outside of the clubhouse and went in to get Mr. Austin's book. At the last minute he had remembered leaving it in his locker.

Linx and all of the Magic Dozen were feeling the excitement of the day. Birdie jumped on top of the locker and started to cheer, "Zack! Zack, he's our man; if he can't do it no one can!" Triple Bogey had rejoined the group thanks to Linx. They had chimed in with make shift pom poms made from scraps of torn up tissue paper. "Zack! Zack, he's our man; if he can't do it no one can!"

All of the Magic Dozen were pumped up and ready to go. Walking out of the locker room Zack turned to Linx and asked, "Didn't I leave my clubs right here, in the bag stand?" Zack pointed to an empty rack.

"You sure did Zack. Right there in the rack next to the door."

"My clubs? Where are they?" asked Zack in a slightly louder than normal voice. He had been heard by several members of the crowd and people started whispering. The news spread rapidly throughout the gallery.

Mr. Austin ran over after hearing the news. "Zack, are you sure you left them right here?"

"Yes, Mr. Austin right here by the locker room door. They're gone!"

"Double check your locker and start asking around," said Mr. Austin. He went back to the tournament desk and made an announcement over the loud speaker.

"There will be a 15 minute delay of the final round of the Junior City Championship. It appears that one of the finalists has misplaced their clubs. They are Ben Hogan clubs. Any information regarding their location should be reported to the tournament desk."

"What am I gonna do?" Zack frantically asked Linx.

"Calm down Zack. We're on it! The others are already searching."

Mr. Barnes and Zack's mother came over to comfort him. "We'll find them Zack. Just try to keep your head in the game."

Mr. Austin walked over to Zack and informed him that at the end of the 15 minutes, he would need to decide whether to forfeit the championship or use another set of clubs. "I am truly sorry Zack, but the rules are clear. I can get you some of our rental clubs if you'd like; they're not your Ben Hogans, but they aren't bad. We will continue looking, but I think you should try and play."

Zack thought for a moment. *I've worked so hard, and now in the final round, my clubs are missing!* "I'll play," Zack said quietly. Frustrated and confused, he took the rental clubs and headed toward the first tee.

"Zack, this is a tough situation, but we have made it through things worse than this. You made it to the finals, Mr. Vogel is awake, and even though these clubs aren't yours, they will work. Just try and get a feel for them as soon as possible. We are going to split up and find your clubs," said Linx.

"All right guys, it's go time! Zack's clubs are missing, and we've got to find them! We know who the obvious suspect is, but we don't know what he did with them. Get creative. Think of everything! After you've scanned every inch of Emerald Pond we'll meet back in the locker room. We'll finish our search there."

"It's going to be ok, Zack, trust me. I'll be back soon," said Linx.

Zack stepped up to the tee box to be introduced. "Ladies and gentlemen, Emerald Pond is proud to present the finalists of the City Junior Championship Tournament. In case of a tie at the end of 18 holes, a sudden death will be played to determine the winner. Good luck gentlemen."

Johnny had won the toss and elected to hit first. He drove his ball down the left side of the fairway, where it rolled to a stop. "Nice clubs, Zack," he said sarcastically as Zack placed a tee in the ground. "I'll have an easy win!" Johnny said. Zack's ball skimmed down the fairway, bouncing several times. Unfortunately, it came up short, and didn't make it as far as Johnny's drive.

The two walked down the fairway, and the crowd followed. Linx made it through the mass of people just as he heard Zack's mother and Mr. Barnes talking to Mr. Beam who had finally arrived at the tournament.

"I am sorry to hear about Zack's clubs. I was really surprised to hear he made it this far. Clearly he's worked hard. Just as long as everything stays fair, you know?" said Mr. Beam.

"What do you mean? Don't you think Zack is playing fair?" Zack's mother asked.

"I'm not saying that. I just don't understand how he got so good, so fast. But as long as everything is honest, then he deserves to be congratulated. Especially since his winning streak will probably end here. Tell him congrats for me, won't you?" said Mr. Beam.

Linx thought hard about the lost clubs. He began by retracing all of the morning's steps. "Zack placed his clubs here and then went inside. He retrieved Mr. Austin's book, came out the door and noticed his clubs were missing. Mr. Austin ran over, Johnny came out and headed for the tee box. Hmmm…That's it!"

Most of the Magic Dozen had already scattered. Wet, Beach, and Birdie were looking to Linx for directions.

"I want you guys to check every single locker in this building. I think that's where we'll find Zack's clubs. Wet come with me. I know Mr. Austin can't hear us, but we have to try anyway. At the very least, we need to be there when he gets to the locker room." The search of the lockers began. The Dozen climbed on top of each other and peered in through the vents. Wet dashed toward the scorekeeper's table.

Linx caught up to Zack on the fourth hole. "Nice day for golf, don't you think?" Linx asked.

"Come on Linx, this is no time for jokes. I can't get a feel for these clubs, and I am already down by five strokes."

"Good, that's what I want to hear, focus. Stay calm and play one shot at a time, review your book, and let your swing just happen. Let the club do the work."

"I'm trying Linx,"

Johnny must have overheard Zack talking with Linx. "Already talking to yourself, huh Zack? Losers usually wait until they're on the back nine before they choke."

The next few holes got worse for Zack.

"I'll be right back," said Linx.

At the clubhouse, Linx walked into a messy scene. Triple Bogey had thrown themselves into a laundry basket of towels. The towels that were scattered all over the floor showed how much fun they were having while looking for the clubs.

Greenie popped his head out of the trash can. After he jumped to the ground, Linx noticed that Greenie's foot was stuck to the floor. "I don't know why Triple Bogey is always playing in the trash. It's dangerous in here. Look at this! Gum! No clubs, but plenty of gum," Greenie complained. Linx laughed as he watched Greenie wrestle the sticky pink wad.

Just then Birdie's song caught Linx's attention, "I found them! We did it guys." Linx followed the sound around the corner. There he saw a Magic Dozen totem pole. Beach was standing firm on the bottom with Mulligan balancing on his head. On top of Mulligan was You Da Man, and then Birdie. Both You Da Man and Birdie could see the clubs.

"Right there! There they are, I can see 'em!" shouted Birdie with a high pitched whistle. Suddenly the locker room door sprang open. Wet was riding on top of Mr. Austin's shoulder.

"I want every locker opened! Search every one. Let's start on the aisles." Mr. Austin announced. He started opening one locker after another with his keys. The other men searched through the lockers one by one.

"Dude! Dude! Over here. Here's the ticket," grunted Beach as he tried to keep his balance. All the balls started pulling on Mr. Austin's pant legs. They were shouting now, trying desperately to get his attention. They hoped against all odds that somehow Mr. Austin could hear them.

Finally Mr. Austin was standing in front of the locker that held the clubs. Linx looked up to read the shining metal plaque on the door. *Jack Beam.*

The locker was opened. Mr. Austin announced, "Well, it appears we've located Zack's clubs." He double-checked the name on the outside of the locker and headed for the course. Mr. Austin could see that Zack and Johnny were walking down the ninth fairway toward the clubhouse. Mr. Austin jumped into a cart and raced toward the crowd. Pulling alongside the gallery, he leaned out of the cart and whispered, "Jack, can I please see you for a moment. We've found the clubs, and now we need to talk." Mr. Beam joined Mr. Austin in the cart and headed back to the clubhouse.

"Care to explain how these clubs got in *your* locker, Jack?" asked Mr. Austin.

"What do you mean? I didn't put them there. I have no clue. You don't think I did this do you?"

"If you expect me to believe you, then I'm going to need to know who else knows your locker combination." stated Mr. Austin.

"Um, well, only Johnny," Jack replied sheepishly.

"I thought maybe," said Mr. Austin. "We will get to the bottom of this later but first, we need to get these clubs to Zack."

Johnny and Zack had just finished the ninth hole when Mr. Austin stopped his cart by the tenth hole tee box. Zack watched Mr. Austin get out of the cart and walk around to the other side and lift out his clubs.

"We found them Zack," Mr. Austin said proudly.

"Where were they?" asked Zack.

"We'll talk about it later," said Mr. Austin, as he peered rigidly at Johnny. "Just go play!"

Zack took a deep breath and tried to refocus on the game. He was far behind at the end of the front nine. Catching up looked impossible. "Linx, there's not enough time for me to win."

"We are *all* here for you and we know you can do it."

"That's right Zack we *believe*," the Magic Dozen chanted. Linx looked over at the group to see that Lost was missing.

"Where's Lost?" asked Linx.

"Who knows," said Wet.

"He'll show up sooner or later," said Greenie.

"Yeah, somehow he always does," said Linx shaking his head.

"All you need to do is birdie seven of the remaining holes and get an eagle," said Long Ball.

"Remember, Johnny started this and we are going to finish it," said Triple Bogey as they cannonballed into Zack's bag.

On the tenth tee Johnny's drive went straight down the middle of the fairway. "Great drive don't you think, Zack?" Johnny said with a smirk. The gallery was not clapping. They too were getting tired of Johnny's attitude.

Zack got ready to swing and noticed Long Ball smiling up at him. *Whack!* The ball rocketed off Zack's club and sailed past Johnny's ball by 80 yards.

Zack hit his next shot with the assistance of Greenie, who was known for laser like precision. The ball rolled to a stop six inches from the cup. Zack tapped the ball into the cup for a birdie and announced, "That's one."

Johnny was still ahead by eight strokes. He continued his sarcastic comments, though they were coming less often as his lead melted.

The next hole was a repeat of the hole before, "That's two," said Zack looking directly at Johnny.

The Magic Dozen, after helping on the last two shots, stepped back. Zack noticed and was glad they were there, but he was not a cheater and knew that if he was going to win, he was going to win fair. The balls were in their element cheering Zack on hole after hole. Zack was catching up. Johnny looked worried. As he worried, Zack's confidence grew with every stroke.

"Come on Zack, just a few more holes," chanted someone in the gallery. Others began clapping.

By the eighteenth hole, Zack had almost caught up. He only needed an eagle to tie with Johnny and force a sudden death playoff.

At the last hole Zack felt certain that Johnny would hit a drive, lay up, and then position for his third shot. Then he would either sink the ball with one putt for a birdie, or if he used two putts then he'd make par. Zack blasted a drive in an attempt to get in position to make the green in two shots for an eagle. Meanwhile, Johnny played it safe and took another stroke.

"You can't make the green in two," said Johnny sarcastically.

"Wait and see," snapped Zack. He had remembered Jeff trying to hit the same shot the day before and knew he had to hit it just right.

"Good Call," said Linx. "Time to take that chance." Zack lined up to the ball. He knew it was going to be quite a stretch.

Zack pulled the club back and let it fly. The ball sailed over the trees, over the protecting sand trap, and landed safely on the green only fifteen feet from the pin.

"Zack's back," chanted the gallery.

Johnny waved at the crowd but no one waved back. Johnny hit his second shot and reached the green with three strokes, just as Zack had predicted. Then Johnny needed to make a 20-foot putt for a birdie.

In the gallery Mr. Barnes and Zack's mother watched nervously. "If Johnny makes this putt, it's all over, no matter what Zack does. If he misses and Zack makes his putt, then we have a sudden death playoff." whispered Mr. Barnes to Zack's mother.

"I can't watch," she said, putting her hands over her eyes.

Johnny walked around the green looking at every angle, trying to get the perfect read. He put his putter in place and tapped the ball. It started tracking directly toward the hole. At the last moment the ball caught the edge of the cup and rolled to the side. The crowd was silent. Not an "oooh" or "ahhh" came from the crowd.

Now it was Zack's turn. If he made it, a sudden death would be played. If he missed, all Johnny needed to do was tap his putt in to win. He slowly took his putter back and started his stroke.

"MISS IT," shouted Johnny. Zack's concentration was broken, but it was too late. His putter jumped and hit the ball before he could stop it. The ball rolled toward the hole, heading for the cup. It seemed to roll in slow motion. Zack felt as if time had sopped. After what seemed an eternity, the ball came to rest at he edge of the cup.

12

Truth

Zack stood motionless, knowing that Mr. Vogel had just lost everything. All of the work, dedication, and practice were for nothing. Zack felt sick to his stomach as his vision blurred. He thought he might pass out. The roar of disappointment from the gallery brought Zack back to the moment.

Zack straightened his shoulders and forced himself to walk over to the cup. He wiped his sweaty palms on his pants, gripped his putter, and tapped his ball into the cup to end the round. *Now what? How am I ever going to face Mr. Vogel? It's over!*

Johnny only needed to make a six inch putt to win. In his frustration, Zack wished he could yell at Johnny the same way he had done to him, but he just couldn't. Johnny was so confident that he didn't bother to read the putt. He smiled at the crowd, pulled back his putter, and let the ball roll. There was no question that the ball was headed straight toward the center of the cup. It was right on line.

Zack felt another wave of nausea roll across his stomach. His shoulders fell. He watched as the ball began to drop in the cup and then unexpectedly bounce out. He rubbed his eyes and shook his head. His thoughts ran wild. *What? How? Wait...*

A small helmet raised out of the cup. "No clubs in here," echoed a muffled voice from inside. As he emerged from the hole, Lost slipped off the side of the cup and rolled back in. "Ouch," echoed the voice again.

Emerald Pond was silent.

All at once the crowd started to roar. Zack and Johnny were tied and would have to play a sudden death match.

Johnny fell to his knees in disbelief. "I've been cheated," he cried. "Zack's a cheater! " No one listened.

Mr. Austin quieted the gallery so Johnny could make his last putt, officially sending the pair into sudden death. He sank the putt.

"Sudden death," announced Mr. Austin. "Back to hole number 18. " The gallery lined the fairway.

"Here's your chance Zack," said Linx with a wink.

"I know."

For a moment everything was quiet. Zack checked to make sure everything was perfect. He wanted to remember this moment forever. Maybe. Zack looked for his mother and saw she was covering her mouth, her eyes wide with excitement. Mr. Barnes was yelling. Zack knew this was it. This was what he had been working towards for five months: the practice, the studying, the exercise, and all the healthy food. Strangely, he felt very calm and in control. He was proud of himself. It was a new feeling and it was good.

Just before the awards ceremony, Zack carefully gathered the Magic Dozen and put them in his backpack. He wanted to have them as close as possible. For the first time since Zack had met them, they had nothing to say. Zack couldn't stop grinning as he left the locker room and headed to the banquet hall where he was awarded the City Junior Tournament Championship trophy.

After the ceremony everyone rushed to the stage to congratulate him. Zack was awarded several invitations from people to play with them. His picture was taken, and he was interviewed for the newspaper. His mother tears kept coming.

Zack saw Jack Beam pull Johnny to the side. In front of everyone, he took Johnny by the arm and led him a few steps away from the crowd.

"I think it's time you tell me exactly *who* put Zack's clubs in my locker."

"It wasn't me dad. I don't know who did it! " Johnny's reply wasn't convincing his father, or the crowd who was straining to hear the conversation.

"It was *you* who put Zack's clubs in my locker and it was *you* and *your* friends that attacked Zack at the range…*you're* a bully!" accused Mr. Beam.

Johnny was not used to his dad questioning him. He had always been able to shift the blame. Johnny's face turned red as he curled his hands into fists.

"OKAY! FINE! I DID IT! SO WHAT! THIS WOULDN'T BE HAPPENING IF THAT STUPID BALL WOULD'VE JUST HIT ZACK LIKE IT WAS SUPPOSED TO INSTEAD OF HITTING MR. VOGEL!" yelled Johnny.

People in the crowd gasped. Mr. Beam stood silent. "Get to the car! You are finished here," he said through clenched teeth. He walked ahead of Johnny, keeping his head down. Johnny threw his clubs and crossed his arms as he marched after his dad.

No one said anything, but all eyes were on Zack. Zack looked around for the closest exit and ran for the locker room. He needed to be alone.

"Linx, it's all my fault! That ball never would have hit Mr. Vogel if he wasn't trying to help me!"

"Zack, you didn't hit Mr. Vogel. It's not your fault. You couldn't have done anything to stop Johnny. Mr. Vogel is recovering, and you've just won the tournament. When Mr. Vogel gets back on his feet, he will be planning the biggest and best golf course this town has ever seen."

Just then Mr. Austin, Mr. Barnes, and Zack's mother came into the locker room. Mr. Austin handed the trophy to Zack. "Let's go! "

"There's someone who is going to want a closer look," said Mr. Barnes. Zack smiled.

Zack couldn't stop himself. He ran down the hallway to Mr. Vogel's room. They had been waiting for this moment for too long. Mr. Vogel's eyes were shut when they entered the room.

"Mr. Vogel, are you awake?"

Mr. Vogel opened one eye first and then the other. A big grin lit up his face.

"How's my Champ?" asked Mr. Vogel.

"Good. How's my Coach? " Mr. Vogel laughed out loud as Zack stood beside the bed holding the trophy. He reached out his hand, and Zack quickly took hold of it. Mr. Vogel raised their hands into the air and said, "You really are a champion."

Back in his bedroom, ready for bed, Zack climbed under the covers. He let his head fall back onto his pillow. On his night stand all of the balls were huddled together talking, laughing, and reminiscing. Zack had become accustomed to their constant chattering. He lay quiet, listening. The balls talked about Lost searching for the clubs inside the hole and having Johnny's ball clock him in the head; Zack joined their laughter. It really had been amazing.

Zack said, "You guys have been the *best*! I don't know what I'd ever do without you."

"Well Zack, you're about to find out," Linx said softly.

"What do you mean? You're not going anywhere."

"Well, that's not exactly true. You see, we've accomplished what we came here to do. That means our time with you is over. Of course we'll never forget you, but we are going to leave."

"LEAVE! You can't! I won't let you! What are you talking about?" cried Zack.

"Look at you, you don't need us anymore. You're strong, confident, and able to tackle whatever faces you in the future. We're proud of you. I'm so sorry to tell you this…but they elected me. " Linx pointed over his shoulder at the rest of the Magic Dozen who sat quietly staring at Zack. "We will be with you tonight, but only until you fall asleep. When you wake up in the morning, we will be gone. Don't forget what you've learned," said Linx.

"Stay positive and work your hardest," said Greenie.

"No matter what it is that you desire to be good at, *practice*!" said Long Ball.

"Take care of your body, keep it healthy. And that means getting plenty of water," Wet said with a big grin.

"Go after *everything* with passion," chimed in Triple Bogey.

"Believe in your ability and be kind," added Birdie.

"Always forgive; especially big mean bullies, like Johnny. They're not very happy laddie, and they need help too," instructed Mulligan.

"Thank the ones who help ya along the way, and be true to those ya call your friends. Most importantly don't forget to have fun, dude!" said Beach.

Zack lay quiet for a few moments with his eyes shut, trying to stop the tears.

"But you guys are my friends. What if I can't remember everything without you here to remind me? I know I'll forget! I'll need you here. Right?"

"You'll remember."

"What will make you stay?" Zack asked.

"We'll be here until you fall asleep. Once you've entered dreamland we will be on our way. There's more teaching to be done and more people who could use our help. I know you've heard about Teena. We want to see what she's been up to and if there's any way that we can help. We're all a team, and we've been gone a long time."

"If you're gonna to be here until I fall asleep, then I just won't go to sleep. I'll stay up all night! I'll never sleep again," insisted Zack.

Linx smiled, along with all the others. They didn't look happy to be leaving either.

For the next few hours the balls and Zack talked. They talked about everything, including the first time they all met Zack. There was plenty of laughing. Especially when they recalled the time that Triple Bogie tied Johnny's shoe laces together, or when Wet splashed Johnny at the water fountain. Finally, Zack laid his head on the pillow and let his eye lids fall shut.

"Good night, Zack," said the Magic Dozen in unison.

"No! No, I'm not sleeping. I'm just gonna rest my eyes for a sec," Zack said slowly. He couldn't fight anymore. Sleep was taking over. Linx whistled and everyone jumped back into the box. Everyone except him. He jumped onto Zack's pillow and whispered, "Ben would have been proud."

Mr. Vogel rolled his wheel chair over the grass. It was difficult getting around, but soon he would be back to using his "trusty 4 iron." It was Mr. Vogel's first day back. "It's great to be back to my old stompin' grounds, Zack! Even if I'm not doin' too much stompin' these days, " Mr. Vogel said as the air filled with his contagious laugh.

Someone interrupted them. "Have you decided where the club house will go?" The two of them turned to see Jack Beam. He had Johnny standing next to him. Johnny was looking down, kicking at a small rock by his foot.

"Hello Mr. Beam," said Mr. Vogel.

"Hello, I'm glad to see that you're out of bed. I plan on upholding up my end of the deal as soon as possible. And I've brought my son who has agreed to help build your famous golf course. Free of charge. You might consider it somewhat of a community service project. He's really excited, aren't you Johnny?"

"Yes sir," Johnny answered quietly.

"I wanted you to know that even after the construction is complete, Johnny can work here after school and on weekends at anything you need him to do. Of course, that's if you'll have him. He won't be playing golf until next summer," informed Mr. Beam.

"That's fine with me, as long as Johnny realizes that I'm not very fun to work for," challenged Mr. Vogel.

"He's not expecting easy work, Mr. Vogel. He is expecting to do exactly what he's told, when he's told. And he has something to say to the both of you."

"I'm sorry," Johnny said as he lifted his head. "I know what I did was bad. Mr. Vogel, I never wanted to hurt you. I guess I did some dumb things. Will you forgive me?"

"I think I can. But, if you're gonna be hanging around I need to know that you've changed. Any sign of the old Johnny, and we're going to have ourselves a problem," said Mr. Vogel.

"I've always been mean to you, Zack. Sorry. Can you forgive me?"

"Yeah, I can," Zack said, after pausing a moment to think about everything the Magic Dozen had taught him.

"We really appreciate your time, and for listening to what my son had to say. You can both rest easy, knowing that he has learned his lesson. This next year will be tough for him. Maybe he can make a total turn around, just like you Zack. Anything is possible, right? " Both Mr. Vogel and Zack smiled. Mr. Beam had *no* idea how true that really was.

As Pop's story finished, Mason looked around. "Wait a minute, are you telling me that *this* is the place? This is what Mr. Beam built for Mr. Vogel?"

"It's true…all of this started with a run-down little driving range, and a very large, very risky bet," Pops said.

"Wow! This place is awesome. I guess Mr. Beam kept his promise."

"You *bet* he did!" They both laughed. Mason felt sad that the story was over. He had enjoyed the entire thing. Time seemed to fly by as Pops shared each detail. "Time to go home Mason. It's getting late. I'm starving. We need to eat and take Hammer for a walk."

They took a walk through the clubhouse, and Pops waved to a few of the men he knew. Outside, Mason jumped in the truck, and they headed back to Pops' house. Mason was quiet for most of the ride.

Mason's thoughts drifted back to Zack. He found himself imagining the Magic Dozen. He laughed a little and said, "Pops, you believe that whole story, except the part about *magic golf balls*, right?"

"Well, that would be silly, wouldn't it?" shrugged Pops.

"Yeah!"

"Couldn't you imagine it though?" Pops questioned.

"If there was a Magic Dozen, then maybe anyone could change, just like Zack," stated Mason.

"Well, yes. But maybe *anyone* could change, just by hearing about them."

Mason slowly shook his head up and down.

At the house Mason threw Hammer's favorite rubber toy for him. Pops made dinner while Mason and Hammer played. After dinner they took Hammer for a walk. Pops asked Mason a question on the way home. "I know I have asked before, but what do you think AJ is doing right now?"

Mason paused before answering, "Maybe he's practicing…"

"I think you're right. Maybe next time you'll have a different response when AJ asks to play?"

"You think he's like Zack don't you?"

"I think anything is possible. I think everyone deserves a chance. I think you just might be the one to give AJ that chance." Pops said.

The day came to a close and evening descended on Pop's house. An unfamiliar feeling surrounded Mason. The day had been wonderful. He was full of hope for school on Monday morning. He would be able to change things for AJ.

After getting ready for bed, Mason hugged Pops and headed down the hallway towards his bedroom. Just before he climbed into bed, he noticed Pop's light was on in his study. From his doorway he was able to see into the room, which was just a few steps away at the end of the hall. He turned away from his bed and walked towards the light.

Inside the study, shelves were lined with books. A large bookcase covered the entire wall on either side of Pops' huge wooden desk. There was an area for writing, a place for his computer, shelves, and drawers. His big brown leather chair was tucked neatly up to the desk. Mason's favorite part of the room was the enormous stone fireplace that covered the entire wall opposite the doorway. Important things stayed on Pops' mantle. Mason remembered Pops showing him a few of the things he always kept there.

Mason hadn't paid too much attention to it. There were a few old trophies. Four books were lying down on their sides, piled on top of each other. Mason assumed these were his favorites. From where he stood he could read the name stretched out on the spines. Mason turned to leave the study, leaning the door shut behind him. It wasn't until he climbed into bed that he realized the name on the books was the same as the name on one of Pop's trophies. He repeated it out loud. "Zackary Mason Stevenson. Zackary Mason Stevenson."

His mind began reeling as he thought back to Pop's story. Was it possible? Mason jumped out of bed and quickly ran to the study. He pushed the door open and squinted in the bright light of the lamp. He stood in front of the mantle and stared. Sitting on top, resting under a pile of books, there was a small white box with the initials HB in the bottom corner…and an old rubber band wrapped tightly around…

About the Authors

Steve Brown, aka "Brown," is the founder and president of Be the Ball, Inc. Brown lives in Salt Lake City with the "Magic Dozen," his donkey, his wife, and her horse, hawk, and hounds. He additionally founded the Be the Ball Foundation whose mission targets the fight against child obesity. For more foundation information, please go to www.betheballfoundation.org. Brown can be reached at sbrown@xmission.com.

Amber Lee Sellers lives with her beautiful family in the Salt Lake Valley of Northern Utah. She is married to Joshua, and together they are raising two wonderful babies. Life consists of writing, photography, and finding inspiration in all the ways God chooses to give it.

For additional retail be the ball products please go to:

www.betheball4u.com
www.tumblersgalore.com